PR  W9-CEJ-546

AN 87TH PRECINCT NOVEL

AND

"Excellent"
Best Sellers

"Familiarity with the cops of the
87th Precinct
breeds something like devotion:
the more we know about them,
the more we want to know.
Their puzzles are our nightmares."
Newsweek

"Simply the best police procedurals
being written in the United States!"
Washington Post Book World

80 MILLION EYES

AN 87TH PRECINCT NOVEL

ED McBAIN

AVON BOOKS NEW YORK

AVON BOOKS
A division of
The Hearst Corporation
105 Madison Avenue
New York, New York 10016

Published by arrangement with HUI Corporation
Library of Congress Catalog Card Number: 86-91642
ISBN: 0-380-70367-X

First Avon Books Printing: May 1987

AVON TRADEMARK REG. U.S. PAT. OFF. AND IN OTHER COUNTRIES, MARCA
REGISTRADA, HECHO EN U.S.A.

Printed in the U.S.A.

RA 10 9 8 7 6 5 4 3

This is for
Judy and Fred Underhill

1

The man was sitting on a bench in the reception room when Miles Vollner came back from lunch that Wednesday afternoon. Vollner glanced at him, and then looked quizzically at his receptionist. The girl shrugged slightly and went back to her typing. The moment Vollner was inside his private office, he buzzed her.

"Who's that waiting outside?" he asked.

"I don't know, sir," the receptionist said.

"What do you mean, you don't know?"

"He wouldn't give me his name, sir."

"Did you ask him?"

"Yes, I did."

"What did he say?"

"Sir, he's sitting right here," the receptionist said, her voice lowering to a whisper. "I'd rather not—"

"What's the matter with you?" Vollner said. "This is *my* office, not *his*. What did he say when you asked him his name?"

"He—he told me to go to hell, sir."

"What?"

"Yes, sir."

"I'll be right out," Vollner said.

He did not go right out because his attention was caught by a letter on his desk, the afternoon mail having been placed there some five minutes ago by his secretary. He opened the letter, read it quickly, and then smiled because

1

it was a large order from a retailer in the Midwest, a firm Vollner had been trying to get as a customer for the past six months. The company Vollner headed was small but growing. It specialized in audio-visual components, with its factory across the River Harb in the next state, and its business and administrative office here on Shepherd Street in the city. Fourteen people worked in the business office—ten men and four women. Two hundred and six people worked in the plant. It was Vollner's hope and expectation that both office and factory staffs would have to be doubled within the next year, and perhaps trebled the year after that. The large order from the Midwest retailer confirmed his beliefs, and pleased him enormously. But then he remembered the man sitting outside, and the smile dropped from his face. Sighing, he went to the door, opened it, and walked down the corridor to the reception room.

The man was still sitting there.

He could not have been older than twenty-three or twenty-four, a sinewy man with a pale narrow face and hooded brown eyes. He was clean-shaven and well dressed, wearing a grey topcoat open over a darker grey suit. A pearl-grey fedora was on top of his head. He sat on the bench with his arms folded across his chest, his legs outstretched, seemingly quite at ease. Vollner went to the bench and stood in front of him.

"Can I help you?" he said.

"Nope."

"What do you want here?"

"That's none of your business," the man said.

"I'm sorry," Vollner answered, "but it is my business. I happen to own this company."

"Yeah?" He looked around the reception room, and smiled. "Nice place you've got."

The receptionist, behind her desk, had stopped typing and was watching the byplay. Vollner could feel her presence behind him.

"Unless you can tell me what you want here," he said, "I'm afraid I'll have to ask you to leave."

The man was still smiling. "Well," he said, "I'm not

about to tell you what I want here, and I'm not about to leave, either."

For a moment, Vollner was speechless. He glanced at the receptionist, and then turned back to the man. "In that case," he said, "I'll have to call the police."

"You call the police, and you'll be sorry."

"We'll see about that," Vollner said. He walked to the receptionist's desk and said, "Miss Di Santo, will you get me the police, please?"

The man rose from the bench. He was taller than he had seemed while sitting, perhaps six feet two or three inches, with wide shoulders and enormous hands. He moved toward the desk and, still smiling, said, "Miss Di Santo, I wouldn't pick up that phone if I was you."

Miss Di Santo wet her lips and looked at Vollner.

"Call the police," Vollner said.

"Miss Di Santo, if you so much as put your hand on that telephone, I'll break your arm. I promise you that."

Miss Di Santo hesitated. She looked again to Vollner, who frowned and then said, "Never mind, Miss Di Santo," and without saying another word, walked to the entrance door and out into the corridor and toward the elevator. His anger kept building inside him all the way down to the lobby floor. He debated calling the police from a pay phone, and then decided he would do better to find a patrolman on the beat and bring him back upstairs personally. It was two o'clock, and the city streets were thronged with afternoon shoppers. He found a patrolman on the corner of Shepherd and Seventh, directing traffic. Vollner stepped out into the middle of the intersection and said, "Officer, I'd—"

"Hold it a minute, mister," the patrolman said. He blew his whistle and waved at the oncoming automobiles. Then he turned back to Vollner and said, "Now, what is it?"

"There's a man up in my office, won't tell us what his business is."

"Yeah?" the patrolman said.

"Yes. He threatened me and my receptionist, and won't leave."

"Yeah?" The patrolman kept looking at Vollner curiously, as though only half-believing him.

"Yes. I'd like you to come up and help me get him out of there."

"You would, huh?"

"Yes."

"And who's gonna handle the traffic on this corner?" the patrolman said.

"This man is threatening us," Vollner said. "Surely that's more important than—"

"This is one of the biggest intersections in the city right here, and you want me to leave it."

"Aren't you supposed to—"

"Mister, don't bug me, huh?" the patrolman said, and blew his whistle, and raised his hand, and then turned and signaled to the cars on his right.

"What's your shield number?" Vollner said.

"Don't bother reporting me," the patrolman answered. "This is my post, and I'm not supposed to leave it. You want a cop, go use the telephone."

"Thanks," Vollner said tightly. "Thanks a lot."

"Don't mention it," the patrolman said breezily, and looked up at the traffic light, and then blew his whistle again. Vollner walked back to the curb and was about to enter the cigar store on the corner, when he spotted a second policeman. Still fuming, he walked to him rapidly and said, "There's a man up in my office who refuses to leave and who is threatening my staff. Now just what the hell do you propose to do about it?"

The patrolman was startled by Vollner's outburst. He was a new cop and a young cop, and he blinked his eyes and then immediately said, "Where's your office, sir? I'll go back there with you."

"This way," Vollner said, and they began walking toward the building. The patrolman introduced himself as Ronnie Fairchild. He seemed brisk and efficient until they entered the lobby, where he began to have his first qualms.

"Is the man armed?" he asked.

"I don't think so," Vollner said.

"Because if he is, maybe I ought to get some help."

"I think you can handle it," Vollner said.

"You think so?" Fairchild said dubiously, but Vollner had already led him into the elevator. They got out of the car on the tenth floor, and again Fairchild hesitated. "Maybe I ought to call this in," he said. "After all . . ."

"By the time you call it in, the man may *kill* someone," Vollner suggested.

"Yeah, I suppose so," Fairchild said hesitantly, thinking that if he *didn't* call this in and ask for help, the person who got killed might very well be himself. He paused outside the door to Vollner's office. "In there, huh?" he said.

"That's right."

"Well, okay, let's go."

They entered the office. Vollner walked directly to the man, who had taken his seat on the bench again, and said, "Here he is, officer."

Fairchild pulled back his shoulders. He walked to the bench. "All right, what's the trouble here?" he asked.

"No trouble, officer."

"This man tells me you won't leave his office."

"That's right. I came here to see a girl."

"Oh," Fairchild said, ready to leave at once now that he knew this was only a case of romance. "If that's all . . ."

"What girl?" Vollner said.

"Cindy."

"Get Cindy out here," Vollner said to his receptionist, and she rose immediately and hurried down the corridor. "Why didn't you tell me you were a friend of Cindy's?"

"You didn't ask me," the man said.

"Listen, if this is just a private matter—"

"No, wait a minute," Vollner said, putting his hand on Fairchild's arm. "Cindy'll be out here in a minute."

"That's good," the man said. "Cindy's the one I want to see."

"Who are you?" Vollner asked.

"Well, who are *you?*"

"I'm Miles Vollner. Look, young man—"

"Nice meeting you, Mr. Vollner," the man said, and smiled again.

"What's your name?"

"I don't think I'd like to tell you that."

"Officer, ask him what his name is."

"What's your name, mister?" Fairchild said, and at that moment the receptionist came back, followed by a tall blond girl wearing a blue dress and high-heeled pumps. She stopped just alongside the receptionist's desk and said, "Did you want me, Mr. Vollner?"

"Yes, Cindy. There's a friend of yours here to see you."

Cindy looked around the reception room. She was a strikingly pretty girl of twenty-two, full-breasted and wide-hipped, her blond hair cut casually close to her head, her eyes a cornflower blue that echoed the color of her dress. She studied Fairchild and then the man in grey. Puzzled, she turned again to Vollner.

"A friend of *mine?*" she asked.

"This man says he came here to see you."

"Me?"

"He says he's a friend of yours."

Cindy looked at the man once more, and then shrugged. "I don't know you," she said.

"No, huh?"

"No."

"That's too bad."

"Listen, what is this?" Fairchild said.

"You're *going* to know me, baby," the man said.

Cindy looked at him coldly, and said, "I doubt that very much," and turned and started to walk away. The man came off the bench immediately, catching her by the arm.

"Just a second," he said.

"Let go of me."

"Honey, I'm *never* gonna let go of you."

"Leave that girl alone," Fairchild said.

"We don't need fuzz around here," the man answered. "Get lost."

Fairchild took a step toward him, raising his club. The man whirled suddenly, planting his left fist in Fairchild's stomach. As Fairchild doubled over, the man unleashed a vicious uppercut that caught him on the point of his jaw and sent him staggering back toward the wall. Groggily, Fairchild reached for his gun. The man kicked him in the groin, and he fell to the floor groaning. The man kicked him again, twice in the head, and then repeatedly in the chest. The receptionist was screaming now. Cindy was running down the corridor, shouting for help. Vollner stood with his fists clenched, waiting for the man to turn and attack him next.

Instead, the man only smiled and said, "Tell Cindy I'll be seeing her," and walked out of the office.

Vollner immediately went to the phone. Men and women were coming out of their private offices all up and down the corridor now. The receptionist was still screaming. Quickly, Vollner dialed the police and was connected with 87th Precinct.

Sergeant Murchison took the call and advised Vollner that he'd send a patrolman there immediately and that a detective would stop by either later that day or early tomorrow morning.

Vollner thanked him and hung up. His hand was trembling, and his receptionist was still screaming.

In another part of the 87th Precinct, on a side street off Culver Avenue, in the midst of a slum as rank as a cesspool, there stood an innocuous-looking brick building that had once served as a furniture loft. It was now magnanimously called a television studio. The Stan Gifford Show originated from this building each and every Wednesday night of the year, except during the summer hiatus.

It was a little incongruous to see dozens of ivy-league, narrow-tied advertising and television men trotting through a slum almost every day of the week in an attempt to put together Gifford's weekly comedy hour. The neighborhood citizens watched the procession of creators with a jaundiced eye; the show had been on the air for three solid years, and they had grown used to seeing these aliens in their midst. There had never been any trouble between the midtown masterminds and the uptown residents, and there probably never would be—a slum has enough troubles without picking on a network. Besides, most of the people in the neighborhood liked the Stan Gifford Show, and would rush indoors the moment it took to the air. If all these nuts were required to put together the show every week, who were they to complain? It was a good show, and it was free.

The good show, and the free one, had been rehearsing since the previous Friday in the loft on North Eleventh, and it was now 3:45 P.M. on Wednesday afternoon, which meant that in exactly four hours and fifteen minutes, a telop would flash in homes across the continent announcing the Stan Gifford Show to follow, and then there would be a station break with commercial, and then the introductory theme music, and then organized bedlam would once again burst forth from approximately twenty million television sets. The network, gratuitously giving itself the edge in selling prime time to potential sponsors, estimated that in each viewing home there were at least two people, which meant that every Wednesday night at 8:00 P.M., eighty million eyes would draw a bead on the smiling countenance of Stan Gifford as he waved from the screen and said, "Back for more, huh?" In the hands of a lesser personality, this opening remark—even when delivered with a smile—might have caused many viewers to switch to another channel or even turn off the set completely. But Stan Gifford was charming, intelligent, and born with an intuitive sense of comedy. He knew what was funny and what was not, and he could even turn a bad joke into a good one simply by acknowledging its failure with a dead-pan nod and a slightly contrite look at his adoring fans. He exuded an ease that seemed totally unrehearsed, a calm that could only be natural.

"Where the hell is Art Wetherley?" he shouted frantically at his assistant director.

"Here just a minute ago, Mr. Gifford," the a.d. shouted back, and then instantly yelled for quiet on the set. The moment quiet was achieved, he broke the silence by shouting, "Art Wetherley! Front and center, on the double!"

Wetherley, a diminutive gag writer who had been taking

a smoke on one of the fire escapes, came into the studio, walked over to Gifford and said, "What's up, Stan?"

Gifford was a tall man, with a pronounced widow's peak—he was actually beginning to bald, but he preferred to think of his receding hairline as a pronounced widow's peak—penetrating brown eyes, and a generous mouth. When he smiled, his eyes crinkled up from coast to coast, and he looked like a youthful, beardless Santa Claus about to deliver a bundle of goodies to needy waifs. He was not smiling now, and Wetherley had seen the unsmiling Gifford often enough to know that his solemn countenance meant trouble.

"Is this supposed to be a joke?" Gifford asked. He asked the question politely and quietly, but there was enough menace in his voice to blow up the entire city.

Wetherley, who could be as polite as anyone in television when he waned to, quietly said, "Which one is that, Stan?"

"This mother-in-law line," Gifford said. "I thought mother-in-law jokes went out with nuclear fission."

"I wish *my* mother-in-law had gone out with nuclear fission," Wetherley said, and then instantly realized this was not a time for adding one bad joke to another. "We can cut the line," he said quickly.

"I don't want it cut. I want a substitute for it."

"That's what I meant."

"Then why didn't you say what you meant?" Gifford looked across the studio at the wall clock, which was busily ticking off minutes to air time. "You'd better hurry," he said. "Stay away from mothers-in-law, and stay away from Liz Taylor, and stay away from the astronauts."

"Gee," Wetherley said, deadpan, "what does that leave?"

"Some people actually think you're funny, you know that?" Gifford said, and he turned his broad back on Wetherley and walked away.

The assistant director, who had been standing near one of the booms throughout the entire conversation, sighed heavily and said, "Boy, I hope he calms down."

"*I* hope he drops dead," Wetherley answered.

*   *   *

Steve Carella watched as his wife poured coffee into his cup. "You're beautiful," he said, but her head was bent over the coffeepot, and she could not see his lips. He reached out suddenly and cupped her chin with his hand, and she lifted her head curiously, a faint half smile on her mouth. He said again, "Teddy, you're beautiful," and this time she watched his lips, and this time she saw the words on his mouth, and understood them and nodded in acknowledgment. And then, as if his voice had thundered into her silent world, as if she had been waiting patiently all day long to unleash a torrent of words, she began moving her fingers rapidly in the deafmute alphabet.

He watched her hands as they told him of the day's events. Behind the hands, her face formed a backdrop, the intense brown eyes adding meaning to each silent word she delivered, the head of black hair cocking suddenly to one side to emphasize a point, the mouth sometimes moving into a pout, or a grimace, or a sudden radiant smile. He watched her hands and her face, interpolating a word or a grunt every now and then, sometimes stopping her when she formed a sentence too quickly, and marveling all the while at the intense concentration in her eyes, the wonderful animation she brought to the telling of the simplest story. When in turn she listened, her eyes watched intently, as if afraid of missing a syllable, her face mirroring whatever was being said. Because she never heard the intonations or subtleties of any voice, her imagination supplied emotional content that sometimes was not there at all. She could be moved to tears or laughter by a single innocuous sentence; she was like a child listening to a fairy tale, her mind supplying every fantastic unspoken detail. As they did the dishes together, their conversation was a curious blend of household plans and petty larceny, problems with the butcher and the lineup, a dress marked down to twelve ninety-five and a suspect's .38-caliber pistol. Carella kept his voice very low. Volume meant nothing to Teddy, and he knew the twins were asleep in the other room. There was a hushed warmth to that kitchen, as if it gently echoed a city that was curling up for the night.

In ten minutes' time, in twenty million homes, forty million people would turn eighty million eyes on a smiling Stan Gifford who would look out at the world and say, "Back for more, huh?"

Carella, who did not ordinarily enjoy watching television, had to admit that he was one of those forty million hopeless unwashed addicts who turned to Gifford's channel every Wednesday night. Unconsciously, he kept one eye on the clock as he dried the dishes. For whatever perverse reasons, he derived great pleasure from Gifford's taunting opening statement, and he would have felt cheated if he had tuned in too late to hear it. His reaction to Gifford surprised even himself. He found most television a bore, an attitude undoubtedly contracted from Teddy, who derived little if any pleasure from watching the home screen. She was perfectly capable of reading the lips of a performer when the director chose to show him in a close shot. But whenever an actor turned his back or moved into a long shot, she lost the thread of the story and began asking Carella questions. Trying to watch her moving hands and the screen at the same time was an impossible task. Her frustration led to his entanglement which in turn led to further frustration, so he had decided the hell with it.

Except for Stan Gifford.

At three minutes to eight that Wednesday night, Carella turned on the television set, and then made himself comfortable in an easy chair. Teddy opened a book and began reading. He watched the final moments of the show immediately preceding Gifford's (a fat lady won a refrigerator) and then read the telop stating STAN GIFFORD IS NEXT, and then watched the station break and commercial (a very handsome, dark-haired man was making love to a cigarette with each ecstatic puff he took), and then there was a slight electronic pause, and Gifford's theme music started.

"Okay if I turn this light lower?" Carella asked. Teddy, her nose buried in her book, did not see him speak. He touched her hand gently, and she looked up. "Okay to dim this light?" he asked again, and she nodded just as Gifford's face filled the screen.

The smile broke like thunder over Mandalay.

"Back for more, huh?" Gifford said, and Carella burst out laughing and then turned down the lights. The single lamp behind Teddy's chair cast a warm glow over the room. Directly opposite it the colder light of the electronic tube threw a bluish rectangle on the floor directly beneath it. Gifford walked to a table, sat, and immediately went into a monologue, his customary manner of opening the show.

"I was talking to Julius the other day," he said immediately, and the line, for some curious reason, brought a laugh from the studio audience as well as from Carella. "He's got a persecution complex, I'll swear to it. An absolute paranoiac." Another laugh. "I said to him, 'Look, Julie—' I call him Julie because, after all, we've known each other for a long time, some people say I'm almost like a son to him. 'Look, Julie,' I said to him, 'what are you getting all upset about? So a lousy soothsayer stops you on the way to the forum and gives you a lot of baloney about the ides of March, why do you let this upset you, huh? Julie baby, the people *love* you.' Well, he turned to me and said, 'Brutus, I know you think I'm being foolish, but . . .'"

And that's the way it went. For ten solid minutes, Gifford held the stage alone, pausing only to garner his laughs, or to deliver his contrite look when a joke fell flat. At the end of the ten minutes he introduced his dance ensemble, which held the stage for another five minutes. He then paraded his first guest, a buxom Hollywood blonde who sang a torch song and did a skit with him, and before anyone at home realized it, the first half of the show was over. Station break, commercial. Carella got a bottle of beer from the refrigerator, and settled down to enjoy the remaining half hour.

Gifford came on to introduce a group of folk singers who sang *Greensleeves* and *Scarlet Ribbons*, a most colorful combination. He walked onto the stage again as soon as they were finished, and then went to work in earnest. His next guest was a male Hollywood personality. The male Hollywood personality seemed to be somewhat at a loss because he could neither sing nor dance nor, according to some critics, even act. But Gifford engaged him in some very high-priced banter for a few minutes, and then personally began a commercial about triple-roasted coffee while the Hollywood visitor went off to change his costume for a promised skit. Gifford finished the commercial and then motioned to someone standing just off camera. A stagehand carried a chair into viewing range. Gifford thanked him with a small bow, and then placed the chair in the center of the enormous, empty stage.

He had been on camera for perhaps five minutes now, a relatively short time, and when he sat in the chair and heaved a weary sigh, everyone was a little surprised. He kept sitting in the chair, saying nothing, doing nothing. There was no music behind him. He was simply a man sitting in a chair in the middle of an empty stage, but Carella felt himself beginning to smile because he knew Gifford was about to do one of his pantomimes. He touched Teddy's arm, and she looked up from her book. ''The pantomime,'' he said, and she nodded, put down her book, and turned her eyes toward the screen.

Gifford continued doing nothing. He simply sat there and looked out at the audience. But he seemed to be watching something in the very far distance. The stage was silent as Gifford kept watching this something in the distance, a something that seemed to be getting closer and closer. Then, suddenly, Gifford got out of the chair, pulled it aside, and watched the something as it roared past him. He wiped his brow, faced his chair in another direction, and sat again. Now he leaned forward. It was coming from the other direction. Closer it came, closer, and again Gifford got up, pulled his chair aside at the last possible moment, and watched the imaginary thing speed past him. He sat again, facing another direction.

Carella burst into laughter as Gifford spotted it coming at him once more. This time, he got out of the chair with a determined and fierce look on his face. He held the chair in front of him like a lion tamer, defying the something to attack. But again at the last moment he pulled out of the way to let the something roar past. It was now on his left.

He turned, whipping the chair around. The camera came in for a tight shot of his perplexed and completely helpless face.

Another look crossed that face.

The camera eye was in tight for the closeup, and it caught the sudden faintness that flashed across the puzzled features. Gifford seemed to sway for an instant, and then he put one hand to his eyes, as if he weren't seeing too clearly, as if the something rushing from the left had taken on real dimensions all at once. He squeezed his eyes shut tightly, and then shook his head, and then staggered back several paces and dropped the chair, just as the something streaked by him.

It was all part of the act, of course. Everyone knew that. But somehow, Gifford's pantomime had taken on a reality that transcended humor. Somehow, there was real confusion in his eyes as he watched the nameless something begin another charge. The camera stayed on him in a tight closeup. Gifford looked directly into the camera, and there was a pathetically pleading look on his face, and suddenly contact was made again, suddenly the audience began laughing. This was the same sweet and gentle man being pursued by a persistent nemesis. This was comedy again.

Carella did not laugh.

Gifford reached down for the chair. The close shot on one camera yielded to a long shot on another camera. His fingers closed around the chair. He righted it, and then sat in it weakly, his head drooping, and again the audience howled, but Carella was leaning forward now, watching Gifford with a deadly cold impersonal fixed stare.

Gifford clutched his abdomen, as if struck there by the invisible juggernaut. He seemed suddenly dizzy, and his face went pale, and he seemed in danger of falling out of the chair. And then, all at once, for eighty million eyes to see, he became violently ill. The camera was caught unaware for a moment. It lingered on his helpless sickness an instant longer, and then suddenly cut away.

Carella stared at the screen numbly as the orchestra struck up a sprightly tune.

2

There were two squad cars and an ambulance parked in the middle of the street when Detective Meyer Meyer pulled up in front of the loft. Five patrolmen were standing before the single entrance to the building, trying valiantly to keep back the crowd of reporters, photographers, and just plain sightseers who thronged the sidewalk. The newspapermen were making most of the noise, shouting some choice Anglo-Saxon phrases at the policemen who had heard it all already and who refused to budge an inch. Meyer got out of the car and looked for Patrolman Genero, who had called the squadroom not five minutes before. He spotted him almost at once, and then elbowed his way through the crowd, squeezing past an old lady who had thrown a bathrobe over her nightgown, "I beg your pardon, ma'am," and then shoving aside a fat man smoking a cigar, "Would you mind getting the hell out of my way?" and finally reaching Genero, who looked pale and tired as he stood guarding the entrance doorway.

"Boy, am I glad to see you!" Genero said.

"I'm glad to see you, too," Meyer answered. "Did you let anyone get by?"

"Only Gifford's doctor and the people from the hospital."

"Who do I talk to in there?"

"The producer of the show. His name's David Krantz. Meyer, it's bedlam in there. You'd think God dropped dead."

15

"Maybe he did," Meyer said patiently, and he entered the building.

The promised bedlam started almost at once. There were people on the iron-runged stairways, and people in the corridor, and they all seemed to be talking at once, and they all seemed to be saying exactly the same thing. Meyer cornered a bright-eyed young man wearing thick-lensed spectacles and said, "Where do I find David Krantz?"

"Who wants to know?" the young man answered.

"Police," Meyer said wearily.

"Oh. Oh! He's upstairs. Third floor."

"Thanks," Meyer said. He began climbing the steps. On the third floor, he stopped a girl in a black leotard and said, "I'm looking for David Krantz."

"Straight ahead," the girl answered. "The man with the mustache."

The man with the mustache was in the center of a circle of people standing under a bank of hanging lights. At least five other girls in black leotards, a dozen or so more in red spangled dresses, and a variety of men in suits, sweaters, and work clothes were standing in small clusters around the wide expanse of the studio floor. The floor itself was covered with the debris of television production: cables, cameras, hanging mikes, booms, dollies, cue cards, crawls, props and painted scenery. Beyond the girls, and beyond the knot of men surrounding the man with the mustache, Meyer could see a hospital intern in white talking to a tall man in a business suit. He debated looking at the body first, decided it would be best to talk to the head man, and broke into the circle.

"Mr. Krantz?"

Krantz turned with an economy and swiftness of movement that was a little startling. "Yes, what is it?" he said, snapping the words like a whip. He was dressed smartly, quietly, neatly. His mustache was narrow and thin. He gave an immediate impression of wastelessness in a vast wasteland.

Meyer, who was pretty quick on the draw himself, immediately flipped open his wallet to his shield. "Detective Meyer, 87th Squad," he said. "I understand you're the producer."

"That's right," Krantz answered. "What now?"

"What do you mean what now, Mr. Krantz?"

"I mean what are the police doing here?"

"Just a routine check," Meyer said.

"For a man who died of an obvious heart attack?"

"Well, I didn't know you were a doctor, Mr. Krantz."

"I'm not. But any fool—"

"Mr. Krantz, it's very hot in here, and I've been working all day, and I'm tired, you know? Don't start bugging me right off the bat. From what I understand—"

"Here we go," Krantz said to the circle of people around him.

"Here we go *where?*" Meyer said.

"If a maiden lady dies of old age in her own bed, every cop in the city is convinced it's homicide."

"Oh? Who told you that, Mr. Krantz?"

"I used to produce a half-hour mystery show. I'm familiar with the routine."

"And what's the routine?"

"Look, Detective Meyer, what do you want from me?"

"I want you to cut it out, first of all. I'm trying to ask some pretty simple questions about what seems to be an accidental—"

"*Seems?* See what I mean?" he said to the crowd.

"Yeah, *seems,* Mr. Krantz. And you're making it pretty difficult. Now if you'd like me to get a subpoena for your arrest, we can talk it over at the station house. It's up to you."

"Now you're kidding, Detective Meyer. You've got no grounds for arresting me."

"Try Section 1851 of the Penal Law," Meyer said flatly. " '*Resisting public officer in the discharge of his duty:* A person who, in any case or under any circumstances not otherwise specially provided for, wilfully resists, delays, or obstructs a public officer in dis—' "

"All right, all right," Krantz said. "You've made your point."

"Then get rid of your yes-men, and let's talk."

The crowd disappeared without a word. In the distance, Meyer could see the tall man arguing violently with the intern in white. He turned his full attention to Krantz and said, "I thought the show had a studio audience."

"It does."

"Well, where are they?"

"We put them all upstairs. Your patrolman said to hold them."

"I want one of your people to take all their names and tell them to go home."

"Can't the police take—"

"I've got a madhouse in the street outside, and only five men to take care of it. Would you mind helping me, Mr. Krantz? I didn't want him dead any more than you did."

"All right, I'll take care of it."

"Thanks. Now, what happened?"

"He died of a heart attack."

"How do you know? Had he ever had one before this?"

"Not that I know of, but—"

"Then let's leave that open for the time begin, okay? What time was it when he collapsed?"

"I can get that for you. Somebody was probably keeping a timetable. Hold it a second. George! Hey, George!"

A man wearing a cardigan sweater and talking to one of the dancers turned abruptly at the sound of his name. He peered around owlishly for a moment, obviously annoyed, trying to locate the person who'd called him. Krantz raised his hand in signal, and the man picked up a battery-powered megaphone from the seat of the chair beside him and, still annoyed, walked toward the two men.

"This is George Cooper, our assistant director," Krantz said. "Detective Meyer."

Cooper extended his hand cautiously. Meyer realized all at once that the scowl on Cooper's face was a perpetual one, a mixed look of terrible inconvenience and unspeakable injury, as if he were a man trying to think in the midst of a revolution.

"How do you do?" he said.

"Mr. Meyer wants to know what time Stan collapsed."

"What do you mean?" Cooper said, making the sentence sound like a challenge to a duel. "It was after the folk singers went off."

"Yes, but what time? Did anybody keep a record?"

"I can run the tape," Cooper said grudgingly. "Do you want me to do that?"

"Please," Meyer said.

"What happened?" Cooper asked. "Is it a heart attack?"

"We don't—"

"What else could it be?" Krantz interrupted.

"Well, I'll run the tape," Cooper said. "You going to be around?"

"I'll be here," Meyer assured him.

Cooper nodded once, briefly, and walked away scowling.

"Who's that arguing with the intern over there?" Meyer asked.

"Carl Nelson," Krantz replied. "Stan's doctor."

"Was he here all night?"

"No. I reached him at home and told him to come over here in a hurry. That was after I'd called the ambulance."

"Get him over here, will you?"

"Sure," Krantz said. He raised his arm and shouted, "Carl? Have you got a minute?"

Nelson broke away from the intern, turned back to hurl a last word at him, and then walked briskly to where Meyer and Krantz were waiting. He was broad as well as tall, with thick black hair greying at the temples. There was a serious expression on his face as he approached, and a high color in his cheeks. His lips were pressed firmly together, as if he had made a secret decision and was now ready to defend it against all comers.

"That idiot wants to move the body," he said immediately. "I told him I'd report him to the AMA if he did. What do you want, Dave?"

"This is Detective Meyer, Dr. Nelson."

Nelson shook hands briefly and firmly. "Are you getting the medical examiner to perform an autopsy?" he asked.

"Do you think I should, Dr. Nelson?"

"Didn't you see the way Stan died?"

"No. How did he die?"

"It was a heart attack, wasn't it?" Krantz said.

"Don't be ridiculous. Stan's heart was in excellent condition. When I arrived here at about nine o'clock, he was experiencing a wide range of symptoms. Labored respiration, rapid pulse, nausea, vomiting. We tried a stomach pump, but that didn't help at all. He went into convulsion at about nine-fifteen. The third convulsion killed him at nine-thirty."

"What are you suggesting, Dr. Nelson?"

"I'm suggesting he was poisoned," Nelson said flatly.

In the phone booth on the third-floor landing, Meyer deposited his dime and then dialed the home number of Lieutenant Peter Byrnes. The booth was hot and smelly. He waited while the phone rang on the other end. Byrnes himself answered, his voice sounding fuzzy with sleep.

"Pete, this is Meyer."

"What time is it?" Byrnes asked.

"I don't know. Ten-thirty, eleven o'clock."

"I must have dozed off. Harriet went to a movie. What's the matter?"

"Pete, I'm investigating this Stan Gifford thing, and I thought I ought to—"

"What Stan Gifford thing?"

"The television guy. He dropped dead tonight, and—"

"What television guy?"

"He's a big comic."

"Yeah?"

"Yeah. Anyway, his doctor thinks we ought to have an autopsy done right away. Because he had a convulsion, and—"

"Strychnine?" Byrnes asked immediately.

"I doubt it. He was vomiting before he went into convulsion."

"Arsenic?"

"Could be. Anyway, I think the autopsy's a good idea."

"Go ahead, ask the m.e. to do it."

"Also, I'm going to need some help on this. I've got some more questions to ask here, and I thought we might get somebody over to the hospital right away. To be there when the body arrives, you see? Get a little action from them.''

''That's a good idea.''

''Yeah, well, Cotton's out on a plant, and Bert was just answering a squeal when I left the office. Could you call Steve for me?''

''Sure.''

''Okay, that's all. I'll ring you later if it's not too late.''

''What time did you say it was?''

Meyer looked at his watch. ''Ten-forty-five.''

''I must have dozed off,'' Byrnes said wonderingly, and then hung up.

George Cooper was waiting for Meyer when he came out of the booth. The same look was on his face, as if he had swallowed something thoroughly distasteful and was allowing his anger to feed his nausea.

''I ran that tape,'' he said.

''Okay.''

''I timed the second half with a stop watch. What do you want to know?''

''When he collapsed.''

Cooper looked sourly at the pad in his hand and said, ''The folk singers went off at eight-thirty-seven. Stan came on immediately afterwards. He was on camera with that Hollywood ham for two minutes and twelve seconds. When the guest went off to change, Stan did the coffee commercial. He ran a little over the paid-for minute, actually a minute and forty seconds. He started his pantomime at eight-forty-one prime fifty-two. He was two minutes and fifty-five seconds into it when he collapsed. That means he was on camera for a total time of seven minutes and seventeen seconds. He collapsed at eight-forty-four prime seventeen.''

''Thanks,'' Meyer said. ''I appreciate your help.'' He started walking toward the door leading to the studio floor. Cooper stepped into his path. His eyes met Meyer's, and he stared into them searchingly.

''Somebody poisoned him, huh?'' he said.

''What makes you think that, Mr. Cooper?''

"They're all talking about it out there."

"That doesn't necessarily make it true, does it?"

"Dr. Nelson says you'll be asking for an autopsy."

"That's right."

"Then you *do* think he was poisoned."

Meyer shrugged. "I don't think anything yet, Mr. Cooper."

"Listen," Cooper said, and his voice dropped to a whisper. "Listen, I . . . I don't want to get anybody in trouble but . . . before the show tonight, when we were rehearsing—" He stopped abruptly. He glanced into the studio. A man in a sports jacket was approaching the hallway, reaching for the package of cigarettes in his pocket.

"Go ahead, Mr. Cooper," Meyer said.

"Skip it," Cooper answered and walked away quickly. The man in the sports jacket came into the hallway. He nodded briefly to Meyer, put the cigarette into his mouth, leaned against the wall, and struck a match. Meyer took out a cigarette of his own, and then said, "Excuse me. Do you have a light?"

"Sure," the man said. He was a small man, with piercing blue eyes and crew-cut hair that gave his face a sharp triangular shape. He struck a match for Meyer, shook it out, and then leaned back against the wall again.

"Thanks," Meyer said.

"Don't mention it."

Meyer walked to where Krantz was standing with Nelson and the hospital intern. The intern was plainly confused. He had answered an emergency call, and now no one seemed to know what they wanted him to do with the body. He turned to Meyer pleadingly, hoping for someone who would forcefully take command of the situation.

"You can move the body," Meyer said. "Take it to the morgue for autopsy. Tell your man one of our detectives'll be down there soon. Carella's his name."

The intern left quickly, before anybody could change his mind. Meyer glanced casually toward the corridor, where the man in the sports jacket was still leaning against the wall, smoking.

"Who's that in the hallway?" he asked.

"Art Wetherley," Krantz answered. "One of our writers."

"Was he here tonight?"

"Sure," Krantz said.

"All right, who else is connected with the show?"

"Where do you want me to start?"

"I want to know who was here tonight, that's all."

"Why?"

"Oh, Mr. Krantz, *please*. Gifford could have died from the noise alone in this place, but there's a possibility he was poisoned. Now who was here tonight?"

"All right, *I* was here. And my secretary. And my associate producer and his secretary. And the unit manager and his secretary. And the—"

"Does everybody have a secretary?"

"Not everybody."

"Let me hear the rest."

Krantz folded his arms, and then began reciting by rote. "The director, and the assistant director. The two Hollywood stars, and the folk singers. Two scenic designers, a costume designer, the booking agent, the choral director, the chorus—seventeen people in it—the orchestra conductor, two arrangers, thirty-three musicians, five writers, four librarians and copyists, the music contractor, the dance accompanist, the choreographer, six dancers, the rehearsal pianist, the lighting director, the audio man, two stage managers, twenty-nine engineers, twenty-seven electricians and stagehands, three network policemen, thirty-five pages, three makeup men, a hair stylist, nine wardrobe people, four sponsors' men, and six guests." Krantz nodded in quiet triumph. "That's who was here tonight."

"What were you trying to do?" Meyer asked. "Start World War III?"

Paul Blaney, the assistant medical examiner, had never performed an autopsy on a celebrity before. The tag on the corpse's wrist told him, as if he had not already been told by Carella and Meyer, who were waiting outside in the corridor, that the man lying on the stainless-steel table was Stan Gifford, the television comedian. Blaney shrugged. A corpse was a corpse, and he was only thankful that this one hadn't been mangled in an automobile accident. He never watched television, anyway. Violence upset him.

He picked up his scalpel.

He didn't like the idea of two detectives waiting outside while he worked. The next thing you knew, they'd be coming into the autopsy room with him and giving their opinions on the proper way to hold a forceps. Besides, he rather resented the notion that a corpse, simply because it was a celebrity corpse, was entitled to preferential treatment—like calling a man in the middle of the goddamn night to make an examination. Oh, sure, Meyer had patiently explained that this was an unusual case and likely to attract a great deal of publicity. And yes, the symptoms certainly seemed to indicate poisoning of some sort, but still Blaney didn't like it.

It smacked of pressure. A man should be allowed to remove a liver or a set of kidneys in a calm, unhurried way. Not with anxious policemen breathing down his neck. The usual routine was to perform the autopsy, prepare the report, and then send it on to the investigating team of detectives. If a homicide was indicated, it was sometimes necessary to prepare additional reports, which Blaney did whenever he felt like it, more often not. These were sent to Homicide North or South, the chief of police, the commander of the detective division, the district commander, and the technical police laboratory. Sometimes, and only when Blaney was feeling in a particularly generous mood, he would call the investigating precinct detective and give him a verbal necropsy report over the phone. But he had never had cops waiting in the corridor before. He didn't like the idea. He didn't like it at all.

Viciously, he made his incision.

In the corridor outside, Meyer sat on a bench alongside one green-tinted wall and watched Carella, who paced back and forth before him like an expectant father. Patiently, Meyer turned his head in a slow cycle, following Carella's movement to the end of the short corridor and back again. He was almost as tall as Carella, but more heavily built, so that he seemed squat and burly, especially when he was sitting.

"How'd Mrs. Gifford take it?" Carella asked.

"Nobody likes the idea of an autopsy," Meyer said. "But I drove out to her house, and told her why we were going ahead, and she agreed it seemed necessary."

"What kind of a woman?"

"Why?"

"If someone poisoned him . . ."

"She's about thirty-eight or thirty-nine, tall, attractive, I guess. It was a little hard to tell. Her mascara was running all over her face." Meyer paused. "Besides, she wasn't at the studio, if that means anything."

"Who *was* at the studio?" Carella asked.

"I had Genero take down all their names before they were released." Meyer paused. "I'll tell you the truth, Steve, I hope this autopsy comes up with a natural cause of death."

"How many people were in the studio?" Carella said.

"Well, I think we can safely discount the studio audience, don't you?"

"I guess so. How many were in the studio audience?"

"Five hundred and sixty."

"All right, let's safely discount them."

"So that leaves everyone who was connected with the show, and present tonight."

"And how many is that?" Carella asked. "A couple of dozen?"

"Two hundred and twelve people," Meyer asked.

The door to the autopsy room opened, and Paul Blaney stepped into the corridor, pulling off a rubber glove the way he had seen doctors do in the movies. He looked at Meyer and Carella sourly, greatly resenting their presence, and then said, "Well, what is it you'd like to know?"

"Cause of death," Meyer said.

"Acute poisoning," Blaney answered flatly.

"Which poison?"

"Did the man have a history of cardiac ailments?"

"Not according to his doctor."

"Mmmmm," Blaney said.

"Well?" Carella said.

"That's very funny because . . . well, the poison was strophanthin. I recovered it in the small intestine, and I automatically assumed—"

"What's strophanthin?"

"It's a drug similar to digitalis, but much more powerful."

"Why'd you ask about a possible cardiac ailment?"

"Well, both drugs are used therapeutically in the treatment of cardiac cases. Digitalis by infusion, usually, and strophanthin intravenously or intramuscularly. The normal dose is very small."

"Of strophanthin, do you man?"

"Yes."

"Is it ever given by pill or capsule?"

"I doubt it. It may have been produced as a pill years ago, but it's been replaced by other drugs today. As a matter of fact, I don't know any doctors who'd normally prescribe it."

"What do you mean?"

"Well, whenever there's a rhythmical disturbance or a structural lesion, digitalis is the more commonly prescribed stimulant. But strophanthin . . ." Blaney shook his head.

"Why not strophanthin?"

"I'm not saying it's *never* used, don't misunderstand me. I'm saying it's *rarely* used. A hospital pharmacy may get a call for it once in five years. A doctor would prescribe it only if he wanted immediate results. It acts much faster than digitalis." Blaney paused. "Are you sure this man didn't have a cardiac history?"

"Positive." Carella hesitated a moment and then said, "Well, what form *does* it come in today?"

"An ampule, usually."

"Liquid?"

"Yes, ready for injection. You've seen ampules of penicillin, haven't you? Similar to that."

"Does it come in powder form?"

"It could, yes."

"What kind of powder?"

"A white crystalline. But I doubt if any pharmacy, even

a hospital pharmacy, would stock the powder. Oh, you might find one or two, but it's rare.''

"What's the lethal dose?" Carella asked.

"Anything over a milligram is considered dangerous. That's one one-thousandth of a gram. Compare that to the fatal dose of digitalis, which is about two and a half grams, and you'll understand what I mean about power.''

"How large a dose did Gifford have?"

"I couldn't say exactly. Most of it, of course, had already been absorbed, or he wouldn't have died. It's not easy to recover strophanthin from the organs, you know. It's very rapidly absorbed, and very easily destroyed. Do you want me to guess?"

"Please," Meyer said.

"Judging from the results of my quantitative analysis, I'd say he ingested at least two full grains.''

"Is that a lot?" Meyer asked.

"It's about a hundred and thirty times the lethal dose.''

"What!''

"Symptoms would have been immediate,'' Blaney said. "Nausea, vomiting, eventual convulsion.''

The corridor was silent for several moments. Then Carella said, "What do you mean by immediate?"

Blaney looked surprised. "Immediate,'' he answered. "What else does immediate mean but immediate? Assuming the poison was injected—''

"He was out there for maybe ten minutes," Carella said, "with the camera on him every second. He certainly didn't—''

"It was exactly seven minutes and seventeen seconds,'' Meyer corrected.

"Whatever it was, he didn't take an injection of strophanthin.''

Blaney shrugged. "Then maybe the poison was administered orally.''

"How?''

"Well . . .'' Blaney hesitated. "I suppose he could have broken open one of the ampules and swallowed the contents.''

"He didn't. He was on camera. You said the dose was enough to bring on immediate symptoms."

"Perhaps not so immediate if the drug were taken orally. We really don't know very much about the oral dose. In tests with rabbits, *forty* times the normal intramuscular dose and *eighty* times the normal intravenous dose proved fatal when taken by mouth. Rabbits aren't humans."

"But you said Gifford probably had a *hundred and thirty* times the normal dose."

"That's my estimate."

"How long would that have taken to bring on symptoms?"

"Minutes."

"How many minutes?"

"Five minutes perhaps. I couldn't say exactly."

"And he was on camera for more than seven minutes. So the poison must have got into him just before he came on."

"I would say so, yes."

"What about this ampule?" Meyer said. "Could it have been dumped into something he drank?"

"Yes, it could have."

"Any other way he could have taken the drug?"

"Well," Blaney said, "if he'd got hold of the drug in powder form somehow, I suppose two grains could have been placed in a gelatin capsule."

"What's a gelatin capsule?" Meyer asked.

"You've seen them," Blaney said. "Vitamins, tranquilizers, stimulants . . . many pharmaceuticals are packaged in gelatin capsules."

"Let's get back to 'immediate' again," Carella said. "Are we still—"

"How long does it take for a gelatin capsule to dissolve in the body?"

"I have no idea. Several minutes, I would imagine. Why?"

"Well, the capsule would have had to dissolve before any poison could be released, isn't that right?"

"Yes, of course."

"So immediate doesn't always mean immediate, does

it? In this case, immediate means after the capsule dissolves.''

''I just told you it would have dissolved within minutes.''

''How *many* minutes?'' Carella asked.

''I don't know. You'll have to check that with the lab.''

''We will,'' Carella said.

3

The man assigned to investigate the somewhat odd incident in Miles Vollner's office was Detective Bert Kling. Early Thursday morning, while Carella and Meyer were still asleep, Kling took the subway down to the precinct, stopped at the squadroom to see if there were any messages for him on the bulletin board, and then bused over to Shepherd Street. Vollner's office was on the tenth floor. The lettering on the frosted-glass door disclosed that the name of the firm was VOLLNER AUDIO-VISUAL COMPONENTS, unimaginative but certainly explicit. Kling opened the door and stepped into the reception room. The girl behind the reception desk was a small brunette, her hair cut in bangs across her forehead. She looked up as Kling walked in, smiled, and said, "Yes, sir, may I help you?"

"I'm from the police," Kling said. "I understand there was some trouble here yesterday."

"Oh, *yes*," the girl said, "there *cetainly was!*"

"Is Mr. Vollner in yet?"

"No, he isn't," the girl said. "Was he expecting you?"

"Well, not exactly. The desk sergeant—"

"Oh, he doesn't usually come in until about ten o'clock," the girl said. "It's not even nine-thirty yet."

"I see," Kling said. "Well, I have some other stops to make, so maybe I can catch him later on in the—"

"Cindy's here, though," the girl said.

"Cindy?"

"Yes. She's the one he came to see."

"What do you mean?"

"The one he *said* he came to see, anyway."

"The assailant, do you mean?"

"Yes. He said he was a friend of Cindy's."

"Oh. Well, look, do you think I could talk to her? Until Mr. Vollner gets here?"

"Sure, I don't see why not," the girl said, and pressed a button in the base of her phone. Into the receiver, she said, "Cindy, there's a detective here to talk about yesterday. Can you see him? Okay, sure." She replaced the receiver. "In a few minutes, Mr. . . ." She let the sentence hang.

"Kling."

"Mr. Kling. She's got someone in the office with her." The girl paused. "She interviews applicants for jobs out at the plant, you see."

"Oh. Is she in charge of hiring?"

"No, our personnel director does all the hiring."

"Then why does she interview—"

"Cindy is assistant to the company psychologist."

"Oh."

"Yes, she interviews all the applicants, you know, and later our psychologist tests them. To see if they'd be happy working out at the plant. I mean, they have to put together these tiny little transistor things, you know, there's a lot of pressure doing work like that."

"I'll bet there is," Kling said.

"Sure, there is. So they come here, and first she talks to them for a few minutes, to try to find out what their background is, you know, and then if they pass the first interview, our psychologist gives them a battery of psychological tests later on. Cindy's work is very important. She majored in psychology at college, you know. Our personnel director won't even consider a man if Cindy and our psychologist say he's not suited for the work."

"Sort of like picking a submarine crew," Kling said.

"What? Oh, yes, I guess it is," the girl said, and smiled. She turned as a man came down the corridor. He seemed pleased and even inspired by his first interview

with the company's assistant psychologist. He smiled at
the receptionist, and then he smiled at Kling and went to
the entrance door, and then turned and smiled at them both
again, and went out.

"I think she's free now," the receptionist said. "Just let
me check." She lifted the phone again, pressed the button,
and waited. "Cindy, is it all right to send him in now?
Okay." She replaced the receiver. "Go right in," she
said. "It's number fourteen, the fifth door on the left."

"Thank you," Kling said.

"Not at all," the girl answered.

He nodded and walked past her desk and into the corridor. The doors on the left-hand side started with the
number eight and then progressed arithmetically down the
corridor. The number thirteen was missing from the row.
In its place, and immediately following twelve, was fourteen. Kling wondered if the company's assistant psychologist was superstitious, and then knocked on the door.

"Come in," a girl's voice said.

He opened the door.

The girl was standing near the window, her back to him.
One hand held a telephone receiver to her ear, the blond
hair pushed away from it. She was wearing a dark skirt
and a white blouse. The jacket that matched the skirt was
draped over the back of her chair. She was very tall, and
she had a good figure and a good voice. "No, John," she
said, "I didn't think a Rorschach was indicated. Well, if
you say so. I'll call you back later, I've got someone with
me. Right. G'bye." She turned to put the phone back onto
its cradle, and then looked up at Kling.

They recognized each other immediately.

"What the hell are *you* doing here?" Cindy said.

"So you're Cindy," Kling said. "Cynthia Forrest. I'll
be damned."

"Why'd they send *you?* Aren't there any other cops in
that precinct of yours?"

"I'm the boss's son. I told you that a long time ago."

"You told me a lot of things a long time ago. Now go
tell your captain I'd prefer talking to another—"

"My lieutenant."

"*Whatever* he is. I mean, *really*, Mr. Kling, I think there's such a thing as adding insult to injury. The way you treated me when my father was killed—"

"I think there was a great deal of misunderstanding all around at that time, Miss Forrest."

"Yes, and mostly on your part."

"We were under pressure. There was a sniper loose in the city—"

"Mr. Kling, *most* people are under pressure *most* of the time. It was my understanding that policemen are civil servants, and that—"

"We are, that's true."

"Yes, well, you were anything *but* civil. I have a long memory, Mr. Kling."

"So do I. Your father's name was Anthony Forrest, he was the first victim in those sniper killings. Your mother—"

"Look, Mr. Kling—"

"Your mother's name is Clarice, and you've got—"

"Clara."

"Clara, right, and you've got a younger brother named John."

"Jeff."

"Jeff, right. You were majoring in education at the time of the shootings—"

"I switched to psychology in my junior year."

"Downtown at Ramsey University. You were nineteen years old—"

"Almost twenty."

"—and that was close to three years ago, which makes you twenty-two."

"I'll be twenty-two next month."

"I see you graduated."

"Yes, I have," Cindy said curtly. "Now if you'll excuse me, Mr. Kling—"

"I've been assigned to investigate this complaint, Miss Forrest. Something of this nature is relatively small potatoes in our fair city, so I can positively guarantee the lieutenant won't put another man on it simply because you don't happen to like my face."

"Among *other* things."

"Yes, well, that's too bad. Would you like to tell me what happened here yesterday?"

"I would like to tell you nothing."

"Don't you want us to find the man who came up here?"

"I do."

"Then—"

"Mr. Kling, let me put this as flatly as I can. I don't like you. I didn't like you the last time I saw you, and I *still* don't like you. I'm afraid I'm just one of those people who never change their minds."

"Bad failing for a psychologist."

"I'm not a psychologist *yet*. I'm going for my master's at night."

"The girl outside told me you're assistant to the company—"

"Yes, I am. But I haven't yet taken my boards."

"Are you allowed to practice?"

"According to the law in this state—I thought you just *might* be familiar with it, Mr. Kling—no one can be licensed to—"

"No, I'm not."

"Obviously. No one can be licensed to practice psychology until he has a master's degree *and* a Ph.D., *and* has passed the state boards. I'm not practicing. All I do is conduct interviews and sometimes administer tests."

"Well, I'm relieved to hear that," Kling said.

"What the hell is that supposed to mean?"

"Nothing," Kling said, and shrugged.

"Look, Mr. Kling, if you stay here a minute longer, we're going to pick up right where we left off. And as I recall it, the last time I saw you, I told you to drop dead."

"That's right."

"So why don't you?"

"Can't," Kling said. "This is my case." He smiled pleasantly, sat in the chair beside her desk, made himself comfortable and very sweetly said, "Do you want to tell me what happened here yesterday, Miss Forrest?"

*   *   *

When Carella got to the squadroom at ten-thirty that morning, Meyer was already there, and a note on his desk told him that a man named Charles Mercer at the police laboratory had called at 7:45 A.M.

"Did you call him back?" Carella asked.

"I just got in a minute ago."

"Let's hope he came up with something," Carella said, and dialed the lab. He asked for Charles Mercer and was told that Mercer had worked the graveyard shift and had gone home at eight o'clock.

"Who's this?" Carella asked.

"Danny Di Tore."

"Would you know anything about the tests Mercer ran for us? On some gelatin capsules?"

"Yeah, sure," Di Tore said. "Just a minute. That was some job you gave Charlie, you know?"

"What'd he find out?"

"Well, to begin with, he had to use a lot of different capsules. They come in different thicknesses, you know. Like all the manufacturers don't make them the same."

"Pick up the extension, will you, Meyer?" Carella said, and then into the phone, "Go ahead, Di Tore."

"And also, there're a lot of things that can affect the dissolving speed. Like if a man just ate, his stomach is full and the capsule won't dissolve as fast. If the stomach's empty, you get a speedier dissolving rate."

"Yeah, go ahead."

"It's even possible for one of these capsules to pass right through the system without dissolving at all. That happens with older people sometimes."

"But Mercer ran the tests," Carella said.

"Yeah, sure. He mixed a batch of five-percent-solution hydrochloric acid, with a little pepsin. To simulate the gastric juices, you know? He poured that into a lot of separate containers and then dropped the capsules in."

"What'd he come up with?"

"Well, let me tell you what he did. He used different brands, you see, and also different sizes. They come in different sizes, you know, the higher the number, the smaller the size. Like a four is smaller than a three, don't ask me.''

''And what'd he find out?''

''They dissolve at different rates of speed, ten minutes, four minutes, eight minutes, twelve minutes. The highest was fifteen minutes, the lowest three minutes. That's a lot of help, huh?''

''Well, it's not exactly what I—''

''But most of them took an average of about six minutes to dissolve. That gives you something to fool around with.''

''Six minutes, huh?''

''Yeah.''

''Okay. Thanks a lot, Di Tore. And thank Mercer, will you?''

''Don't mention it. It kept him awake.''

Carella replaced the phone on its cradle and turned to Meyer.

''So what do you think?''

''What am I, a straight man? What *else* can I think? Whether Gifford drank it, or swallowed it, it had to be just before he went on.''

''Had to be. The poison works within minutes, and the capsule takes approximately six minutes to dissolve. He was on for seven.''

''Seven minutes and seventeen seconds,'' Meyer corrected.

''You think he took it knowingly?''

''Suicide?''

''Could be.''

''In front of forty million people?''

''Why not? There's nothing an actor likes better than a spectacular exit.''

''Well, maybe,'' Meyer said, but he didn't sound convinced.

''We'd better find out who was with him just before he went on.''

''That should be very simple,'' Meyer said. ''Only two hundred and twelve people were there last night.''

"Let's call your Mr. Krantz. Maybe he'll be able to help us."

Carella dialed Krantz's office and asked to talk to him. The switchboard connected him with a receptionist, who in turn connected him with Krantz's secretary, who told him that Krantz was out, would he care to leave a message? Carella asked her to wait a moment, and then covered the mouthpiece.

"Are we going out to see Gifford's wife?" he asked Meyer.

"I think we'd better," Meyer said.

"Please tell Mr. Krantz that he can reach me at Mr. Gifford's home, will you?" Carella said, and then he thanked her and hung up.

Larksview was perhaps a half hour outside the city, an exclusive suburb that miraculously managed to provide its homeowners with something more than the conventional sixty-by-a-hundred plots. In a time of encroaching land development, it was pleasant and reassuring to enter a community of wide rolling lawns, of majestic houses set far back from quiet winding roads. Detective Meyer Meyer had made the trip to Larksview the night before, when he felt it necessary to explain to Melanie Gifford why the police wanted to do an autopsy, even though her permission was not needed. But now, patiently and uncomplainingly, he made the drive again, seeing the community in daylight for the first time, somehow soothed by its well-ordered, gentle terrain. Carella had been speculating wildly from the moment they left the city, but he was silent now as they pulled up in front of a pair of stone pillars set on either side of a white gravel driveway. A half-dozen men with cameras and another half-dozen with pads and pencils were shouting at the two Larksview patrolmen who stood blocking the drive. Meyer rolled down the window on his side of the car and shouted, "Break it up there! We want to get through."

One of the patrolmen moved away from the knot of newspapermen and walked over to the car. "Who are *you,*

Mac?'' he said to Meyer, and Meyer showed him his shield.

"87th Precinct, huh?'' the patrolman said. "You handling this case?''

"That's right,'' Meyer said.

"Then why don't you send some of your own boys out on this driveway detail?''

"What's the matter?'' Carella said, leaning over. "Can't you handle a couple of reporters?''

"A couple? You shoulda seen this ten minutes ago. The crowd's beginning to thin out a little now.''

"Can we get through?'' Meyer asked.

"Yeah, sure, go ahead. Just run right over them. We'll sweep up later.''

Meyer honked the horn, and then stepped on the gas pedal. The newspapermen pulled aside hastily, cursing at the sedan as its tires crunched over the gravel.

"Nice fellas,'' Meyer said. "You'd think they'd leave the poor woman alone.''

"The way *we're* doing, huh?'' Carella said.

"This is different.''

The house was a huge Georgian Colonial, with white clapboard siding and pale-green shutters. Either side of the door was heavily planted with big old shrubs that stretched beyond the boundaries of the house to form a screen of privacy for the back acres. The gravel driveway swung past the front door and then turned upon itself to head for the road again, detouring into a small parking area to the left of the house before completing its full cycle. Meyer drove the car into the parking space, pulled up the emergency brake, and got out. Carella came around from the other side of the car, and together they walked over the noisy gravel to the front door. A shining brass bell pull was set in the jamb. Carella took the knob and yanked it. The detectives waited. Carella pulled the knob again. Again, they waited.

"The Giffords have help, don't they?'' Carella said, puzzled.

"If you were making half a million dollars a year, wouldn't you have help?''

"I don't know," Carella said. *"You're* making fifty-five hundred a year, and Sarah doesn't have help."

"We don't want to seem ostentatious," Meyer said. "If we hired a housekeeper, the commissioner might begin asking me about all that graft I've been taking."

"You too, huh?"

"Sure. Cleared a cool hundred thousand in slot machines alone last year."

"My game's white slavery," Carella said. "I figure to make—"

The door opened.

The woman who stood there was small and Irish and frightened. She peered out into the sunshine and then said, in a very small voice, with a faint brogue, "Yes, what is it, please?"

"Police department," Carella said. "We'd like to talk to Mrs. Gifford."

"Oh." The woman looked more distressed than ever. "Oh, yes," she said. "Yes, come in. She's out back with the dogs. I'll see if I can find her. Police, did you say?"

"That's right, ma'am," Carella said. "If she's out back, couldn't we just go around and look for her?"

"Oh," the woman said. "I don't know."

"You *are* the housekeeper?"

"Yes, sir, I am."

"Well, *may* we walk around back?"

"All right, but—"

"Do the dogs bite?" Meyer asked cautiously.

"No, they're very gentle. Besides, Mrs. Gifford is with them."

"Thank you," Carella said. They turned away from the door and began walking on the flagstone path leading to the rear of the house. A woman appeared almost the moment they turned the corner of the building. She was coming out of a small copse of birch trees set at the far end of the lawn, a tall blond woman wearing a tweed skirt, loafers, and a blue cardigan sweater, looking down at the ground as two golden retrievers ran ahead of her. The dogs saw the detectives almost immediately and began barking.

The woman raised her head and her eyes curiously, and then hesitated a moment, her stride breaking.

"That's Melanie Gifford," Meyer whispered.

The dogs were bounding across the lawn in enormous leaps. Meyer watched their approach uneasily. Carella, who was a city boy himself, and unused to seeing jungle beasts racing across open stretches of ground, was certain they would leap at his jugular. He was, in fact, almost tempted to draw his pistol when the dogs stopped some three feet away and began barking in furious unison.

"Shhh!" Meyer said, and he stamped his foot on the ground. The dogs, to Carella's immense surprise, turned tail and ran yelping back to their mistress, who walked directly toward the detectives now, her head high, her manner openly demanding.

"Yes?" she said. "What is it?"

"Mrs. Gifford?" Carella asked.

"Yes?" The voice was imperious. Now that she was closer, Carella studied her face. The features were delicately formed, the eyes grey and penetrating, the brows slightly arched, the mouth full. She wore no lipstick. Grief seemed to lurk in the corners of those eyes, and on that mouth; grief sat uninvited and omnipresent on her face, robbing it of beauty. "Yes?" she said again, impatiently.

"We're detectives, Mrs. Gifford," Meyer said. "I was here last night. Don't you remember?"

She studied him for several seconds, as if in disbelief. The goldens were still barking, courageous now that they were behind her skirts. "Yes, of course," she said at last, and then added, "Hush, boys," to the dogs, who immediately fell silent.

"We'd like to ask you some questions, Mrs. Gifford," Carella said. "I know this is a trying time for you, but—"

"That's quite all right," she answered. "Would you like to go inside?"

"Wherever you say."

"If you don't mind, may we stay out here? The house . . . I can't seem to . . . it's open out here, and fresh. After what happened . . ."

Carella, watching her, had the sudden notion she was

acting. A slight frown creased his forehead. But immediately, she said, "That sounds terribly phony and dramatic, doesn't it? I'm sorry. You must forgive me."

"We understand, Mrs. Gifford."

"Do you really?" she asked. A faint sad smile touched her unpainted mouth. "Shall we sit on the terrace? It won't be too cool, will it?"

"The terrace will be fine," Carella said.

They walked across the lawn to where a wide flagstone terrace adjoined the rear doors of the house, open to the woods alive with autumn color. There were white wrought-iron chairs and a glass-topped table on the terrace. Melanie pulled a low white stool from beneath the table and sat. The detectives pulled up chairs opposite her, sitting higher than Melanie, looking down at her. She turned her face up pathetically, and again Carella had the feeling that this, too, was carefully staged, that she had deliberately placed herself in a lower chair so that she would appear small and defenseless. On impulse, he said, "Are you an actress, Mrs. Gifford?"

Melanie looked surprised. The grey eyes opened wide for a moment, and then she smiled the same wan smile and said, "I used to be. Before Stan and I were married."

"How long ago were you married, Mrs. Gifford?"

"Six years."

"Do you have any children?"

"No."

Carella nodded. "Mrs. Gifford," he said, "we're primarily interested in learning about your husband's behavior in the past few weeks. Did he seem despondent, or overworked, or troubled by anything?"

"No, I don't think so."

"Was he the type of man who confided things to you?"

"Yes, we were very close."

"And he never mentioned anything that was troubling him?"

"No. He seemed very pleased with the way things were going."

"What things, Mrs. Gifford?"

"The show, the new stature he'd achieved in television.

He'd been a night-club comic before the show went on the air, you know.''

"I didn't know that."

"Yes. Stan started in vaudeville many years ago, and then drifted into night-club work. He was working in Vegas, as a matter of fact, when they approached him to do the television show."

"And it's been on the air how many years now?"

"Three years."

"How old was your husband, Mrs. Gifford?"

"Forty-eight."

"And how old are you?"

"Thirty-seven."

"Was this your first marriage?"

"Yes."

"Your husband's?"

"Yes."

"I see. Would you say you were happily married, Mrs. Gifford?"

"Yes. Extremely happy."

"Mrs. Gifford," Carella said flatly, "do you think your husband committed suicide?"

Without hesitation, Melanie said, "No."

"You know he was poisoned, of course?"

"Yes."

"If you don't think he killed himself, you must think—"

"I think he was murdered. Yes."

"Who do you think murdered him, Mrs. Gifford?"

"I think—"

"Excuse me, ma'am," the voice said from the opened French doors leading to the terrace. Melanie turned. Her housekeeper stood there apologetically. "It's Dr. Nelson, ma'am."

"On the telephone?" Melanie said, rising.

"No ma'am. He's here."

"Oh." Melanie frowned. "Well, ask him to join us, won't you?" She sat immediately. "Again," she said.

"What?"

"He was here last night. Came over directly from the show. He's terribly worried about my health. He gave me

a sedative and then called twice this morning.'' She folded
her arms across her knees, a slender graceful woman who
somehow made the motion seem awkward. Carella watched
her in silence for several moments. The terrace was still.
On the lawn, one of the golden retrievers began barking at
a laggard autumn bird.

"You were about to say, Mrs. Gifford?"

Melanie looked up. Her thoughts seemed to be elsewhere.

"We were discussing your husband's alleged murder."

"Yes. I was about to say I think Carl Nelson killed
him."

4

Dr. Carl Nelson came onto the terrace not two minutes after Melanie had spoken his name, going first to her and kissing her on the cheek, and then shaking hands with Meyer, whom he had met the night before. He was promptly introduced to Carella, and he acknowledged the introduction with a firm handclasp and a repetition of the name, "Detective Carella," with a slight nod and a smile, as if he wished to imprint it on his memory. He turned immediately to Melanie then, and said, "How are you, Mel?"

"I'm fine, Carl," she said. "I told you that last night."

"Did you sleep well?"

"Yes."

"This has been very upsetting," Nelson said. "I'm sure you gentlemen can understand."

Carella nodded. He was busy watching the effect Nelson seemed to be having on Melanie. She had visibly withdrawn from him the moment he stepped onto the terrace, folding her arms across her chest, hugging herself as though threatened by a strong wind. The pose was assuredly a theatrical one, but it seemed genuine nonetheless. If she was not actually frightened of this tall man with the deep voice and the penetrating brown eyes, she certainly appeared suspicious of him; and the suspicion seemingly forced her to turn inward, to flee into icy passivity.

"Was the autopsy conducted?" Nelson asked Meyer.

"Yes, sir."

44

"May I ask what the results were? Or are they classified?"

"Mr. Gifford was killed by a large dose of strophanthin," Carella said.

"Strophanthin?" Nelson looked honestly surprised. "That's rather unusual, isn't it?"

"Are you familiar with the drug, Dr. Nelson?"

"Yes, of course. That is, I know of it. I don't think I've ever prescribed it, however. It's rarely used, you know."

"Dr. Nelson, Mr. Gifford wasn't a cardiac patient, was he?"

"No. I believe I told that to Detective Meyer last night. Certainly not."

"He wasn't taking digitalis or any of the related glycosides?"

"No, sir."

"What *was* he taking?"

"What do you mean?"

"Was he taking any drugs?"

Nelson shrugged. "No. Not that I know of."

"Well, you're his personal physician. If anyone *would* know, it'd be you, isn't that so?"

"That's right. No, Stan wasn't taking any drugs. Unless you want to count headache tablets and vitamin pills."

"What kind of headache tablets?"

"An empirin-codeine compound."

"And the vitamins?"

"B-complex with vitamin C."

"How long had he been taking the vitamins?"

"Oh, several months. He was feeling a little tired, run-down, you know. I suggested he try them."

"You prescribed them?"

"*Prescribed* them? No." Nelson shook his head. "He was taking a brand called PlexCin, Mr. Carella. It can be purchased at any drugstore without a prescription. But I *suggested* it to him, yes."

"You suggested this specific brand?"

"Yes. It's manufactured by a reputable firm, and I've found it to be completely relia—"

"Dr. Nelson, how are these vitamins packaged?"

"In a capsule. Most vitamins are."

"How large a capsule?"

"An O capsule, I would say. Perhaps a double O."

"Dr. Nelson, would you happen to know whether or not Mr. Gifford was in the habit of taking his vitamins during the show?"

"Why, no, I . . ." Nelson paused. He looked at Carella and then turned to Melanie, and then looked at Carella again. "You certainly don't think . . ." Nelson shrugged. "But then, I suppose anything's possible."

"What were *you* thinking, Dr. Nelson?"

"That perhaps someone substituted strophanthin for the vitamins?"

"Would that be possible?"

"I don't see why not," Nelson said. "The PlexCin capsule is an opaque gelatin that comes apart in two halves. I suppose someone could conceivably have opened the capsule, removed the vitamins, and replaced them with strophanthin." He shrugged again. "But that would seem an awfully long way to go to . . ." He stopped.

"To what, Dr. Nelson?"

"Well . . . to murder someone, I suppose."

The terrace was silent again.

"Did he take these vitamin capsules every day?" Carella asked.

"Yes," Nelson answered.

"Would you know *when* he took them yesterday?"

"No, I—"

"*I* know when," Melanie said.

Carella turned to her. She was still sitting on the low stool, still hugging herself, still looking chilled and lost and forlorn.

"When?" Carella asked.

"He took one after breakfast yesterday morning." Melanie paused. "I met him for lunch in town yesterday afternoon. He took another capsule then."

"What time was that?"

"Immediately after lunch. About two o'clock."

Carella sighed.

"What is it, Mr. Carella?" Melanie asked.

"I think my partner is beginning to hate clocks," Meyer said.

"What do you mean?"

"You see, Mrs. Gifford, it takes six minutes for a gelatin capsule to dissolve, releasing whatever's inside it. And strophanthin acts immediately."

"Then the capsule he took at lunch couldn't have contained any poison."

"That's right, Mrs. Gifford. He took it at two o'clock, and he didn't collapse until about eight-fifty-five. That's a time span of almost seven hours. No, the poison *had* to be taken while he was at the studio."

Nelson looked thoughtful for a moment. "Then wouldn't it be wise to question—" he began, and stopped speaking abruptly because the telephone inside was ringing furiously, shattering the afternoon stillness.

David Krantz was matter-of-fact, businesslike, and brief. His voice fairly crackled over the telephone wire.

"You called me?" he asked.

"Yes."

"How's Melanie?"

"She seems fine."

"You didn't waste any time getting over there, did you?"

"We try to do our little jobs," Carella said drily, remembering Meyer's description of his encounter with Krantz, and wondering whether everybody in television had such naturally nasty tone of voice.

"What is it you want?" Krantz said. "This phone hasn't stopped ringing all morning. Every newspaper in town, every magazine, every *cretin* in this city wants to know exactly what happened last night! How do *I* know what happened?"

"You were there, weren't you?"

"I was up in the sponsor's booth. I only saw it on the monitor. What do you want from me? I'm very busy."

"I want to know exactly where Stan Gifford was last night before he went on camera for the last time."

"How do I know where he was? I just told you I was up in the sponsor's booth."

"Where does he usually go when he's off camera, Mr. Krantz?"

"That depends on how much time he has."

"Suppose he had the time it took for some folk singers to sing two songs?"

"Then I imagine he went to his dressing room."

"Can you check that for me?"

"Whom would you like me to check it with? Stan's dead."

"Look, Mr. Krantz, are you trying to tell me that in your well-functioning, smoothly oiled organization, *nobody* has any idea where Stan Gifford was while those singers were on camera?"

"I didn't say that."

"What did you say? I'm sure I misunderstood you."

"I said *I* didn't know. I was up in the sponsor's booth. I went up there about fifteen minutes before air time."

"All right, Mr. Krantz, thank you. You've successfully presented your alibi. I assume that Gifford did not come up to the sponsor's booth at any time during the show?"

"Exactly."

"Then you couldn't have poisoned him, isn't that your point?"

"I wasn't trying to establish an alibi for myself. I simply—"

"Mr. Krantz, who *would* know where Gifford was? Would somebody know? Would *anybody* in you organization know?"

"I'll check on it. Can you call me later?"

"I'd rather stop by. Will you be in your office all day?"

"Yes, but—"

"There are some further questions I'd like to ask you."

"About what?"

"About Gifford."

"Am I a suspect in this damn thing?"

"Did I say that, Mr. Krantz?"

"No, I said it. Am I?"

"Yes, Mr. Krantz, you are," Carella said, and hung up.

*   *   *

On the way back to the city, Meyer was peculiarly silent. Carella, who had spelled him at the wheel, glanced at him and said, "Do you want to hit Krantz now or after lunch?"

"After lunch," Meyer said.

"You seem tired. What's the matter?"

"I think I'm coming down with something. My head feels stuffy."

"All that clean, fresh suburban air," Carella said.

"No, I must be getting a cold."

"I can see Krantz alone," Carella said. "Why don't you go on home?"

"No, it's nothing serious."

"I mean it. I can handle—"

"Stop it already," Meyer said. "You'll make me *meshugah*. You sound just like my mother used to. You'll be asking me if I got a clean handkerchief next."

"You got a clean handkerchief?" Carella asked, and Meyer burst out laughing. In the middle of the laugh, he suddenly sneezed. He reached into his back pocket, hesitated, and turned to Carella.

"You see that?" he said. "I *haven't* got a clean handkerchief."

"My mother taught me to use my sleeve," Carella said.

"All right, may I use your sleeve?" Meyer said.

"What'd you think of our esteemed medical man?"

"Is there any Kleenex in this rattletrap?"

"Try the glove compartment. What'd you think of Dr. Nelson?"

Meyer reached into the glove compartment, found a box of tissues, and blew his nose resoundingly. He sniffed again, said, "Ahhhhhh," and then immediately said, "I have a thing about doctors, anyway, but this one I *particularly* dislike."

"How come?"

"He looks like a smart movie villain," Meyer said.

"Which means we can safely eliminate him as a suspect, right?"

"There's a better reason than that for eliminating him.

He was home during the show last night.'' Meyer paused. ''On the other hand, he's a doctor, and would have access to a rare drug like strophanthin.''

''But he was the one who suggested an autopsy, remember?''

''Right. Another good reason to forget all about him. If you just poisoned somebody, you're not going to tell the cops to look for poison, are you?''

''A smart movie villain might do just that.''

''Sure, but then a smart movie cop would instantly know the smart movie villain was trying to pull a swiftie.''

''Melanie Wistful seems to think he did it,'' Carella said.

''Melanie Mournful, you mean. Yeah. I wonder why?''

''We'll have to ask her.''

''I wanted to, but Carl Heavy wouldn't quit the scene.''

''We'll call her later. Make a note.''

''Yes, sir,'' Meyer said. He was silent for a moment, and then he said, ''This case stinks.''

''Give me a good old-fashioned hatchet murder any day.''

''Poison is a woman's weapon as a rule, isn't it?'' Meyer asked.

''Sure,'' Carella said. ''Look at history. Look at all the famous prisoners. Look at Neill Cream and Carlyle Harris. Look at Roland B. Molineux. Look at Henri Landru, look at . . .''

''All right, already, I get it,'' Meyer said.

Lieutenant Peter Byrnes read Kling's report that Thursday afternoon, and then buzzed the squadroom and asked him to come in. When he arrived, Byrnes offered him a chair (which Kling accepted) and a cigar (which Kling declined) and then lighted his own cigar and blew out a wreath of smoke and said, ''What's this 'severe distaste for my personality' business?''

Kling shrugged. ''She doesn't like me, Pete. I can't say I blame her. I was going through a bad time. Well, what am I telling you for?''

"Mmm," Byrnes said. "You think there's anything to this prison possibility?"

"I doubt it. It was a chance, though, so I figured we had nothing to lose." He looked at his watch. "She ought to be down at the BCI right this minute, looking through their pictures."

"Maybe she'll come up with something."

"Maybe. As a follow-up, I called some of the families of Redfield's other victims. I haven't finished them all yet, still a few more to go. But the ones I reached said there'd been no incidents, no threats, nothing like that. I was careful about it, Pete, don't worry. I told them we were making a routine follow-up. I didn't want to alarm them."

"Yeah, good," Byrnes said. "But you don't feel there's a revenge thing working here, is that it?"

"Well, if there is, it'd have to be somebody Redfield knew before we caught him, or somebody he met in stir. Either way, why should anybody risk his own neck for a dead man?"

"Yeah," Byrnes said. He puffed meditatively on his cigar, and then glanced at the report again. "Four teeth knocked out, and three broken ribs," he said. "Tough customer."

"Well, Fairchild's a new cop."

"I know that. Still, this man doesn't seem to have much respect for the law, does he?"

"To put it mildly," Kling said, smiling.

"Your report says he grabbed the Forrest girl by the arm."

"That's right."

"I don't like it, Bert. If this guy can be so casual about beating up a cop, what'll he do if he gets the girl alone sometime?"

"Well, that's the thing."

"I think we ought to get him."

"Sure, but who is he?"

"Maybe we'll get a make downtown. From those mug shots."

"She promised to call in later, as soon as she's had a look."

POLICE DEPARTMENT	COMPLAINT REPORT **COPY**	DETECTIVE SQUAD 87th
CRIME CLASSIFICATION **Assault**		PRECINCT 87th
		COMPLAINT NUMBER 306B-41-11
		DATE OF THIS REPORT 10/14

NAME OF COMPLAINANT SURNAME **Vollner** FIRST NAME AND INITIALS **Miles S.**	ADDRESS OF COMPLAINANT **1116 Shepherd Street**
DATE AND TIME OF OCCURRENCE **October 13** TIME **2 P.M.**	PLACE OF OCCURRENCE **Same as above**
DATE AND TIME REPORTED BY THE COMPLAINANT **10/13** **2:30 P.M.**	DETECTIVE ASSIGNED **Bertram Kling**

DETAILS:

INTERROGATION OF MILES VOLLNER AND CYNTHIA FORREST:

Miles Vollner is president of Vollner Audio-Visual Components at 1116 Shepherd Street. He states that when he returned from lunch at about one forty-five p.m. on Wednesday, October 13th to find a man sitting in his reception room. The man refused to give his name or state his business, and thereafter threatned Mr. Vollner's receptionist (Janice Di Santo) when Vollner asked her to call the police. Vollner promptly went down to the street and enlisted the aid of Patrolman Ronald Fairchild, shield number 36-104, 87th Precinct, who accompanied him back to the office. When confronted by Fairchild, the man stated that he had come there to see a girl, and when asked which girl, he said, "Cindy." (Cindy is the nickname for Miss Cynthia Forrest, who is assistant to the company psychologist.)

Vollner sent for Miss Forrest who looked at the man and claimed she did not know him. When she attempted to leave, the man grabbed her by the arm, at which point Fairchild warned him to leave her alone, moving toward him and raising his club. The man attacked Fairchild, kicking him repeatedl in the head and chest after he fell to the floor. Fairchild was later sent to Buena Vista Hospital. Four teeth had been kicked out of his mouth, and he had suffered three broken ribs. Vollner states he ad never before seen the man, and Miss Forrest states so, too.

Miss Forrest is the daughter of the deceased Anthony Forrest (DD Reports 201A-46-01 through 201A-46-31) first victim of the sniper killings two years agoxx six months ago. Check of records show that Lewis Redfield was tried and convicted first degree murder, sentenced to death in the electric chair, executed at Castleview Penitentiary last March. There seems to be no connection between this case and the sniper murders, but have arranged for Miss Forrest to look at mug shots of any prisoners serving time at Castleview (during Redfield's imprisonment there) and subsequently released. Doubt if this will come up with a make since Redfield was in the death house for entire length of term before execution, although he may have had some contact with general prison population and arranged for harrassment of Miss Forrest and other survivors of his victims.

Miss Forrest's previous contact with me on sniper case has left severe distaste for my personality. If subsequent investigation is indicated, I respectfully submit that case be truned over to someone else on the squad.

Bertram Kling

Detective 3rd/Grade Bertram Kling

''Maybe we'll be lucky.''

''Maybe.''

''If we're not, I think we ought to smoke out this guy. I don't like cops getting beat up, that's to begin with. And I don't like the idea of this guy maybe waiting to jump on that girl. He knocked out four of Fairchild's teeth and broke three of his ribs. Who knows what he'd do to a helpless little girl?''

''She's about five-seven, Pete. Actually, that's pretty big. For a girl, I mean.''

''Still. If we're not careful here, we may wind up with a homicide on our hands.''

''Well, that's projecting a little further than I think we have to, Pete.''

''Maybe, maybe not. I think we ought to smoke him out.''

''How?''

''Well, I'm not sure yet. What are you working on right now?''

''Those liquor-store holdups. And also an assault.''

''When was the last holdup?''

''Three nights ago.''

''What's your plan?''

''He seems to be hitting them in a line, Pete, straight up Culver Avenue. I thought I'd plant myself in the next store up the line.''

''You think he's going to hit again so soon?''

''They've been spaced about two weeks apart so far.''

''Then there's no hurry, right?''

''Well, he may change the timetable.''

''He may change the pattern, too. In which case, you'll be sitting in the wrong store.''

''That's true. I just thought—''

''Let it wait. What's the assault?''

''Victim is a guy named Vinny Marino, he's a small-time pusher, lives on Ainsley Avenue. About a week ago, two guys pulled up in a car and got out with baseball bats. They broke both his legs. The neighborhood rumble is that he was fooling around with one of their wives. That's why they went for his legs, you see, so he wouldn't be able to chase around any more. It's only coincidental that he's a pusher.''

''For my part, they could have killed him,'' Byrnes said. He took his handkerchief from his back pocket, blew his nose, and then said, ''Mr. Marino's case can wait, too. I want you to stay with this one, Bert.''

''I think we'd do better with another man. I doubt if I'll be able to get any cooperation at all from her.''

''Who can I spare?'' Byrnes asked. ''Willis and Brown are on that knife murder, Hawes is on a plant of his own, Meyer and Carella are on this damn television thing, Andy Parker—''

''Well, maybe I can switch with one of them.''

''I don't like cases to change hands once they've been started.''

''I'll do whatever you say, Pete, but—''

''I'd appreciate it,'' Byrnes said.

''Yes, sir.''

''You can follow up the vendetta possibility if you like, but I agree with you. It'll probably turn out to be a dead end.''

''I know. I just felt—''

''Sure, it was worth a try. See where it goes. Contact the rest of those survivors, and listen to what the Forrest girl has to say when she calls later on. But I wouldn't bank on anything along those lines, if I were you.'' Byrnes paused, puffed on his cigar, and then said, ''She claims she doesn't know him, huh?''

''That's right.''

''I thought maybe he was an old boy friend.''

''No.''

''Rejected, you know, that kind of crap.''

''No, not according to her.''

''Maybe he just wants to get in her pants.''

''Maybe.''

''Is she good-looking?''

''She's attractive, yes. She's not a raving beauty, but I guess she's attractive.''

''Then maybe that's it.''

''Maybe, but why would he go after her in this way?''

"Maybe he doesn't *know* any other way. He sounds like a hood, and hoods take what they want. He doesn't know from candy or flowers. He sees a pretty girl he wants, so he goes after her—even if it means beating her up to get her. That's my guess."

"Maybe."

"And that's in our favor. Look what happened to Fairchild when he got in this guy's way. He knocked out his teeth and broke his ribs. *Whatever* he wants from this girl—and it's my guess all he wants is her tail—he's not going to let anybody stop him from getting it, law or otherwise. That's where you come in."

"What do you mean?"

"That's how we smoke him out. I don't want to do anything that'll put this girl in danger. I want this punk to make his move against *you*, Bert."

"Me?"

"You. He knows where she works, and chances are he knows where she lives, and I'll bet my life he's watching her every minute of the day. Okay, let's give him something to watch."

"Me?" Kling said again.

"You, that's right. Stay with that girl day and night. Let's—"

"Day and *night?*"

"Well, with reason. Let's get this guy so goddamn sore at you that he comes after you and tries to do exactly what he did to Fairchild."

Kling smiled. "Gee," he said, "suppose he succeeds?"

"Fairchild is a new cop," Byrnes said. "You told me so yourself."

"Okay, Pete, but you're forgetting something, aren't you?"

"What's that?"

"The girl doesn't like me. She's not going to take kindly to the idea of spending time with me."

"Ask her if she'd rather get raped some night in the elevator after this guy has knocked out her teeth and broken some of her ribs. Ask her that."

Kling smiled again. "She might prefer it."

"I doubt it."

"Pete, she hates me. She *really* . . ."

Byrnes smiled. "Win her over, boy," he said. "Just win her over, that's all."

David Krantz worked for a company named Major Broadcasting Associates, which had its offices downtown on Jefferson Street. Major Broadcasting, or MBA as it was familiarly called in the industry, devoted itself primarily to the making of filmed television programs, but every now and then it ventured into the production of a live show. The Stan Gifford Show was—or at least had been—one of the three shows they presented live from the city each week. A fourth live show was produced bi-monthly on the Coast. MBA was undoubtedly the giant of the television business, and since success always breeds contempt, it had been given various nicknames by disgruntled and ungrateful industry wags. These ranged from mild jibes like Money Banks Anonymous, through gentle epithets like Mighty Bloody Assholes, to genuinely artistic creations like Master Bullshit Artists. Whatever you called the company, and however you sliced it, it was important and vast and accounted for more than sixty percent of the nation's television fare each week.

The building on Jefferson Street was owned by MBA, and featured floor after floor of wood-paneled offices, ravishing secretaries and receptionists exported from the Coast, and solemn-looking young men in dark suits and ties, white shirts, and black shoes and socks. David Krantz was a solemn-looking man wearing the company uniform, but he wasn't as young as he used to be. His secretary showed Meyer and Carella into the office, and then closed the door gently behind them. "I've met Mr. Meyer," Krantz said, a trace of sarcasm in his voice, "but I believe you and I have only had the pleasure on the telephone, Mr. Caretta."

"Carella."

"Carella, forgive me. Sit down, won't you. I'm expecting a call on the tieline, so if I have to interrupt our chat, I know you'll understand."

"Certainly," Carella said.

Krantz smoothed his mustache. "Well, what is it you want to know?"

"First, did you find out where Gifford went while he was off camera?"

"I haven't been able to locate George Cooper. He's our a.d., he's the man who'd know."

"What's an a.d.?" Carella asked.

"Assistant director," Meyer said. "I talked to him last night, Steve. He's the one who timed that tape for me."

"Oh."

"I tried to reach him at home," Krantz said, "but no one answered the phone. I'll try it again, if you like."

"Where does he live?" Carella asked.

"Downtown, in The Quarter. It's his responsibility to see that everyone's in on cue. I'm sure he would know just where Stan went while the folk singers were on. Shall I have my secretary try him again?"

"Please," Carella said.

Krantz buzzed for his secretary. In keeping with company policy, she was a tall and beautiful redhead wearing a tight green sweater and skirt. She listened attentively as Krantz told her to try Cooper's number again, and then said, "We're ready on that call to the Coast now, Mr. Krantz."

"Thank you," Krantz said. "Excuse me," he said to Carella and Meyer, and then he lifted the receiver. "Hello, Krantz here. Hello, Frank, what is it? *Who?* The *writer?* What do you *mean*, the writer? The *writer* doesn't like the changes that were made? Who the hell asked him for his opinion? Well, I *know* he wrote the script, what difference does that make? Just a second now, start from the beginning, will you? Who made the changes? Well, he's a perfectly capable producer, why should the writer have any complaints? He says *what?* He says it's his script, and he resents a half-assed producer tampering with it? Listen, who *is* this fellow, anyway? Who? I never heard of him. What's he done before? The *Saturday Review* says what? Well, what the hell's some literary intelligentsia magazine got to do with the people who watch television? What do I

care if he's a novelist, can he write television scripts? Who
hired him, anyway? Was this cleared here, or was it a
Coast decision? Don't give me any of that crap, Frank,
novelists are a dime a dozen. Yeah, even *good* novelists.
It's the guy who can write a decent television script that's
hard to find. You say he *can* write a decent television
script? Then what's the problem? Oh, I see. He doesn't
like the changes that were made. Well, what changes *were*
made, Frank, can you tell me that? I see, um-huh, the
prostitute was rewritten as a nun, um-huh, I see, and she
doesn't die at the end, she performs a miracle instead,
um-huh, well, how about the hero? Not a truck driver any
more, huh? Oh, I see, he's a football coach now, I get it.
Um-huh, works at the college nearby the church, um-huh.
Is it still set in London? Oh, I see. I see, yes, you want to
shoot it at UCLA, sure, that makes sense, a lot closer to
the studio. Well, gee, Frank, off the top of my head, I'd
say the revisions have made it a much better script, I don't
know what the hell the writer's getting excited about.
Explain to him that the changes are really minor and that
large stretches of his original dialogue and scenes are
intact, just the way he wrote them. Tell him we've had
pressure from the network, and that this necessitated a few
minor—no, use the word 'transitional'—a few transitional changes that were made by a competent producer
because there simply wasn't time for lengthy consultations
about revisions. Tell him we have the highest regard for
his work, and that we're well aware of what the *Saturday
Review* said about him, but explain that we're all in the
same goddamn ratrace, and what else can we do when
we're pressured by networks and sponsors and deadlines?
Ask him to be reasonable, Frank. I think he'll understand.
Fine. Listen, what did the pregnant raisin tell the police?
Well, go ahead, guess. Nope. Nope. She said, 'I was
graped!' " Krantz burst out laughing. "Okay, Frank, I'll
talk to you. Right. So long.''

He hung up. The door to his office opened a second
afterward, and the pretty redhead paused in the doorframe
and said, "I still can't reach Mr. Cooper."

"Keep trying him," Krantz said, and the girl went out.

"I'm sorry about the interruption, gentlemen. Shall we continue?"

"Yes," Carella said. "Can you tell me who was in that booth with you last night?"

"You want the names?"

"I'd appreciate them."

"I anticipated you," Krantz said. "I had my secretary type up a list right after you called this morning."

"That was very thoughtful of you," Carella said.

"In this business, I try to anticipate *everything*."

"It's a pity you couldn't have anticipated Gifford's death," Carella said.

"Yeah, well, that was unforeseen," Krantz said absolutely straight-faced, shaking his head solemnly. "I'll have my secretary bring in that list." He pushed a button on his phone. "She used to work for our head of production out at the studio. Did you ever see tits like that before?"

"Never," Carella said.

"They're remarkable," Krantz said.

The girl came into the office. "Yes, sir?"

"Bring in that list you typed for me, would you? How're you doing with Mr. Cooper?"

"I'll try him again, sir."

"Thank you."

"Yes, sir," she said and went out.

"Remarkable," Krantz said.

"While she's getting the list," Carella said, "why don't you fill us in, Mr. Krantz?"

"Sure. Gladine was in the booth with me, she's usually there to take any notes I might—"

"Gladine?"

"My secretary. The tits," Krantz said. He gestured with his hands.

"Oh. Sure."

"My associate producer was up there, too. Dan Hollis is his name, he's been with MBA for close to fifteen years."

"Who was minding the store?" Meyer asked.

"What do you mean?"

"If you and your associate were in the sponsor's booth—"

"Oh. Well, our unit manager was down on the floor,

and our director was in the control booth, of course, and
our assistant director was making sure everyone—''

"I see, okay," Meyer said. "Who else was in the
sponsor's booth with you?"

"The others were guests. Two of them were sponsors'
representatives; one was a Hollywood director who's shoot-
ing a feature for the studio and who thought Gifford might
be right for a part; and the other two were—''

The door opened.

"Here's that list, sir," Gladine said. "We're trying Mr.
Cooper now."

"Thank you, Gladine."

"Yes, sir," she said, and walked out. Krantz handed
the typewritten list to Carella. Carella looked at the list,
and then passed it to Meyer.

"Mr. and Mrs. Feldensehr, who are they?" Meyer asked.

"Friends of Carter Bentley, our unit manager. He in-
vited them in to watch the show."

"That's all, then, huh? You and your secretary, your
associate Dan Hollis . . . Who's this Nathan Crabb?"

"The Hollywood director. I told you, he—''

"Yes, fine, and Mr. and Mrs. Feldensehr, and are these
last two the sponsor's men?"

"That's right."

"Eight people in all," Carella said. "And five of them
were guests."

"That's right."

"You told us there were *six* guests, Mr. Krantz."

"No, I said five."

"Mr. Krantz," Meyer said, "last night you told me
there were *six*."

"I must have meant Gladine."

"Your secretary?" Carella said.

"Yes. I must have included her as one of the guests."

"That's a little unusual, isn't it, Mr. Krantz? Including
an employee of the company as a guest?"

"Well . . ."

There was a long silence.

"Yes?" Carella said.

"Well . . ."

There was another silence.

"We may be investigating a homicide here, Mr. Krantz," Meyer said softly. "I don't think it's advisable to hide anything from us at this point, do you?"

"Well, I . . . I suppose I can trust you gentlemen to be discreet."

"Certainly," Carella said.

"Nathan Crabb? The director? The one who was here to look at Stan, see if he was right for—"

"Yes?"

"He had a girl with him, the girl he's grooming for his next picture. I deliberately left her name off the list."

"Why?"

"Well, Crabb is a married man with two children. I didn't think it wise to include the girl's name."

"I see."

"I can have it added to the list, if you like."

"Yes, we'd like that," Carella said.

"What time did you go up to the sponsor's booth?" Meyer asked suddenly.

"Fifteen minutes before the show started," Krantz said.

"At seven-forty-five?"

"That's right. And I stayed there right until the moment Stan got sick."

"Who was there when you arrived?"

"Everyone but Crabb and the girl."

"What time did they get there?"

"About five minutes later. Ten to eight—around then."

The door to Krantz's office opened suddenly. Gladine smiled and said, "We've reached Mr. Cooper, sir. He's on oh-three."

"Thank you, Gladine."

"Yes, sir," she said, and went out.

Krantz picked up the phone. "Hello," he said, "Krantz here. Hello, George, I have some policemen in my office, they're investigating Stan's death. They wanted to ask you some questions about his exact whereabouts during the show last night. Well, hold on, I'll let you talk to one of them. His name's Capella."

"Carella."

"Carella, I'm sorry. Here he is, George."

Krantz handed the phone to Carella. "Hello, Mr. Cooper," Carella said. "Are you at home now? Do you expect to be there for a while? Well, I was wondering if my partner and I might stop by. As soon as we leave here. Fine. Would you let me have the address, please?" He took a ballpoint pen from his inside jacket pocket, and began writing the address on an MBA memo slip. "Fine," he said again. "Thank you, Mr. Cooper, we'll see you in a half hour or so. Goodbye." He handed the phone back to Krantz, who replaced it on the cradle.

"Is there anything else I can do for you?" Krantz asked.

"Yes," Meyer said. "You can ask your secretary to get us the addresses and phone numbers of everyone who was in the sponsor's booth when you went up there last night."

"Why? Are you going to check to see that I *really* went up there fifteen minutes before the show?"

"And *remained* there until Gifford collapsed, right?"

"Right," Krantz said. He shrugged. "Go ahead, check it. I'm telling the exact truth. I have nothing to hide."

"We're sure you haven't," Carella said pleasantly. "Have her call us with the information, will you?" He extended his hand, thanked Krantz for his time, and then walked out past Gladine's desk, Meyer following him. When they got to the elevator, Meyer said, "Re*mark*able!"

The Quarter was all the way downtown, jammed into a minuscule portion of the city, its streets as crowded as a bazaar. Jewelry shops, galleries, bookstores, sidewalk cafes, espresso joints, pizzerias, paintings on the curb, bars, basement theaters, art movie houses, all combined to give The Quarter the flavor, if not the productivity, of a real avant-garde community. George Cooper lived on the second floor of a small apartment building on a tiny, twisting street. The fire escapes were hung with flowerpots and brightly colored serapes, the doorways were painted pastel oranges and greens, the brass was polished, the whole street had been conceived and executed by the people who dwelt in it, as quaintly phony as a blind con man.

They knocked on Cooper's door and waited. He answered it with the same scowling expression Meyer had come to love the night before.

"Mr. Cooper?" Meyer said. "You remember me, don't you?"

"Yes, come in," Cooper said. He scowled at Meyer, whom he knew, and then impartially scowled at Carella, who was a stranger.

"This is Detective Carella."

Cooper nodded and led them into the apartment. The living room was sparsely furnished, a narrow black couch against one wall, two black Bertoia chairs against another, the decorating scheme obviously planned to minimize the furnishings and emphasize the modern paintings that hung facing each other on the remaining two walls. The detectives sat on the couch. Cooper sat in one of the chairs opposite them.

"What we'd like to know, Mr. Cooper, is where Stan Gifford went last night while those folk singers were on," Carella said.

"He went to his dressing room," Cooper answered without hesitation.

"How do you know that?"

"Because that's where I went to cue him later on."

"I see. Was he alone in the dressing room?"

"No," Cooper said.

"Who was with him?"

"Art Wetherley. And Maria Vallejo."

"Wetherley's a writer," Meyer explained to Carella. "Who's Maria—what's her name?"

"Vallejo. She's our wardrobe mistress."

"And they were both with Mr. Gifford when you went to call him?"

"Yes."

"Would you know how long they were with him?"

"No."

"How long did *you* stay in the dressing room, Mr. Cooper?"

"I knocked on the door, and Stan said, 'Come in,' and I opened the door, poked my head inside and said, 'Two minutes, Stan,' and he said, 'Okay,' and I waited until he came out.''

"Did he come out immediately?''

"Well, almost immediately. A few seconds. You can't kid around on television. Everything's timed to the second, you know. Stan knew that. Whenever he was cued, he came.''

"Then you really didn't spend any time at all in the dressing room, did you, Mr. Cooper?''

"No. I didn't even go inside. As I told you, I just poked my head in.''

"Were they talking when you looked in?''

"I think so, yes.''

"They weren't arguing or anything, were they?''

"No, but . . .'' Cooper shook his head.

"What is it, Mr. Cooper?''

"Nothing. Would you fellows like a drink?''

"Thanks, no,'' Meyer said. "You're sure you didn't hear anyone arguing?''

"No.''

"No raised voices?''

"No.'' Cooper rose. "If you don't mind, I'll have one. It's not too early to have one, is it?''

"No, go ahead,'' Carella said.

Cooper walked into the other room. They heard him pouring his drink, and then he came back into the living room with a short glass containing ice cubes and a healthy triple shot of whiskey. "I hate to drink so damn early in the afternoon,'' he said. "I was on the wagon for a year, you know. How old do you think I am?''

"I don't know,'' Carella said.

"Twenty-eight. I look older than that, don't I?''

"No, I wouldn't say so,'' Carella said.

"I used to drink a lot,'' Cooper explained, and then took a swallow from the glass. The scowl seemed to vanish from his face at once. "I've cut down.''

"When Mr. Gifford left the dressing room,'' Meyer said, "you were with him, right?''

"Yes.''

"Did you meet anyone between the dressing room and the stage?"

"Not that I remember. Why?"

"Would you remember if you'd met anyone?"

"I think so, yes."

"Then the last people who were with Gifford were Art Wetherley, Maria Vallejo, and you. In fact, Mr. Cooper, if we want to be absolutely accurate, the very *last* person was *you*."

"I suppose so. No, wait a minute. I think he said a word to one of the cameramen, just before he went on. Something about coming in for the close shot. Yes, I'm sure he did."

"Did Mr. Gifford eat anything in your presence?"

"No."

"Drink anything?"

"No."

"Put anything into his mouth at all?"

"No."

"Was he eating or drinking anything when you went into the dressing room?"

"I didn't *go* in, I only *looked* in. I think maybe there were some coffee containers around. I'm not sure."

"They were drinking coffee?"

"I told you, I'm not sure."

Carella nodded and then looked at Meyer and then looked at Cooper, and then very slowly and calmly said. "What is it you want to tell us, Mr. Cooper?"

Cooper shrugged. "Anything you want to know."

"Yes, but specifically."

"I don't want to get anybody in trouble."

"What is it, Mr. Cooper?"

"Well . . . well, Stan had a fight with Art Wetherley yesterday. Just before the show. Not a fight, an argument. Words. And . . . I said something about I wished Stan would calm down before we went on the air, and Art . . . Look, I don't want to get him in trouble. He's a nice guy, and I wouldn't even mention this, but the papers said Stan was poisoned and . . . well, I don't know."

"What did he say, Mr. Cooper?"

"He said he wished Stan would drop dead."

Carella was silent for a moment. He rose then and said, "Can you tell us where Mr. Wetherley lives, please?"

Cooper told them where Wetherley lived, but it didn't matter very much because Wetherley was out when they got there. They checked downstairs with his landlady, who said she had seen him leaving the building early this morning, no he didn't have any luggage with him, why in the world would he be carrying luggage at ten o'clock in the morning? Carella and Meyer told the landlady that perhaps he would be carrying luggage if he planned to leave the city, and the landlady told them he never left the city on Thursday because that was when MBA ran the tape of the show from the night before so the writers could see which jokes had got the laughs and which hadn't, and that was very important in Mr. Wetherley's line of work. Carella and Meyer explained that perhaps, after what had happened last night, the tape might not be run today. But the landlady said it didn't matter what had happened last night, they'd probably get a replacement for the show, and then Mr. Wetherley would have to write for it, anyway, so it was very important that he see the tape today and know where the audience laughed and where it didn't. They thanked her, and then called MBA, who told them the tape was not being shown today and no, Wetherley was not there.

They had coffee and crullers in a diner near Wetherley's apartment, debated putting out a Pickup-and-Hold on him, and decided that would be a little drastic on the basis of hearsay, assuming Cooper was telling the truth to begin with—which he might not have been. They were knowledgeable and hip cops and they knew all about this television ratrace where people slit each others' throats, and stabbed each other in the back. It was, after all, quite possible that *everybody* was lying. So they called the squadroom and asked Bob O'Brien to put what amounted to a telephone surveillance on Wetherley's apartment, calling him every half hour, and warning him to stay right in that apartment where he was, in case he happened to answer the phone. O'Brien had nothing else to do but call

Wetherley's apartment every half hour, being involved in trying to solve three seemingly related Grover Park muggings, so he was naturally very happy to comply with Carella's wishes. The two detectives discussed how large a tip they should leave the waitress, settled on a trifle more than fifteen percent because she was fast and had good legs, and then went out into the street again.

The late afternoon air was crisp and sharp, the city vibrated with a shimmering clarity that caused buildings to leap out from the sky. The streets seemed longer, stretching endlessly to a distant horizon that was almost visible. The landmarks both men had grown up with, the familiar sights that gave the city perspective and reality, seemed to surround them intimately now, seemed closer and more intricately detailed. You could reach out to touch them, you could see the sculptured stone eye of a gargoyle twelve stories above the street. The people, too, the citizens who gave a city its tempo and its pace, walked with their topcoats open, no longer faceless, contagiously enjoying the rare autumn day, filling their lungs with air that seemed so suddenly sweet. Carella and Meyer crossed the avenue idly, both men smiling. They walked together with the city between them like a beautiful young girl, sharing her silently, somewhat awed in her radiant presence.

For a little while at least, they forgot they were investigating what looked like a murder.

5

As Kling had anticipated, Cindy Forrest was not over-whelmed by the prospect of having to spend even an infinitesimal amount of time with him. She reluctantly admitted, however, that such a course might be less repulsive than the possibility of spending an equal amount of time in a hospital. It was decided that Kling would pick her up at the office at noon Friday, take her to lunch, and then walk her back again. He reminded her that he was a city employee and that there was no such thing as an expense account for taking citizens to lunch while trying to protect them, a subtlety Cindy looked upon as simply another index to Kling's personality. Not only was he obnoxious, but he was apparently cheap as well.

Thursday's beautiful weather had turned foreboding and blustery by Friday noon. The sky above was a solemn grey, the streets seemed dimmer, the people less animated. He picked her up at the office, and they walked in silence to a restaurant some six blocks distant. She was wearing high heels, but the top of her head still came only level with his chin. They were both blond, both hatless. Kling walked with his hands in his coat pockets. Cindy kept her arms crossed over her middle, her hands tucked under them. When they reached the restaurant, Kling forgot to hold open the door for her, but only the faintest flick of Cindy's blue eyes showed that this was exactly what she expected from a man like him. Too late, he allowed her to precede him into the restaurant.

"I hope you like Italian food," he said.

"Yes, I do," she answered, "but you might have asked *first*."

"I'm sorry, but I have a few other things on my mind besides worrying about which restaurant you might like."

"I'm sure you're a very busy man," Cindy said.

"I am."

"Yes, I'm sure."

The owner of the restaurant, a short Neapolitan woman with masses of thick black hair framing her round and pretty face, mistook them for lovers and showed them to a secluded table at the rear of the place. Kling remembered to help Cindy off with her coat (she mumbled a polite thank you) and then further remembered to hold out her chair for her (she acknowledged this with a brief nod). The waiter took their order and they sat facing each other without a word to say.

The silence lengthened.

"Well, I can see this is going to be perfectly charming," Cindy said. "Lunch with you for the next God knows how long."

"There are things I'd prefer doing myself, Miss Forrest," Kling said. "But, as you pointed out yesterday, I am only a civil servant. I do what I'm told to do."

"Does Carella still work up there?" Cindy asked.

"Yes."

"I'd much rather be having lunch with him."

"Well, those are the breaks," Kling said. "Besides, he's married."

"I know he is."

"In fact, he's got two kids."

"I know."

"Mmm. Well, I'm sure he'd have loved this choice assignment, but unfortunately he's involved with a poisoning at the moment."

"Who got poisoned?"

"Stan Gifford."

"Oh? Is he working on that? I was reading about in the paper just yesterday."

"Yes, it's his case."

"He must be a good detective. I mean, to get such an important case."

"Yes, he's very good," Kling said.

The table went silent again. Kling glanced over his shoulder toward the door, where a thickset man in a black overcoat was just entering.

"Is that your friend?" he asked.

"No. And he's *not* my friend."

"The lieutenant thought he might have been one of your ex-boy friends."

"No."

"Or someone you'd met some place."

"No."

"You're sure you didn't recognize any of those mug shots yesterday?"

"I'm positive. I don't know who the man is, and I can't imagine what he wants from me."

"Well, the lieutenant had some ideas about that, too."

"What were his ideas?"

"Well, I'd rather not discuss them."

"Why not?"

"Because . . . well, I'd just rather not."

"Is it the lieutenant's notion that this man wants to lay me?" Cindy asked.

"What?"

"I said is it the—"

"Yes, something like that," Kling answered, and then cleared his throat.

"I wouldn't be surprised," Cindy said.

The waiter arrived at that moment, sparing Kling the necessity of further comment. Cindy had ordered the antipasto to start, a supposed specialty of the house. Kling had ordered a cup of minestrone. He carefully waited for her to begin eating before he picked up his spoon.

"How is it?" he asked her.

"Very good." She paused. "How's the soup?"

"Fine."

They ate in silence for several moments.

"What *is* the plan exactly?" Cindy asked.

"The lieutenant thinks your admirer is something of a hothead, a reasonable assumption, I would say. He's hoping we'll be seen together, and he's hoping our man will take a crack at me."

"In which case?"

"In which case I will crack him back and carry him off to jail."

"My hero," Cindy said drily, and attacked an anchovy on her plate.

"I'm supposed to spend as much time with you as I can," Kling said, and paused. "I guess we'll be having dinner together tonight."

"What?"

"Yes," Kling said.

"Look, Mr. Kling—"

"It's not *my* idea, Miss Forrest."

"Suppose I've made other plans?"

"Have you?"

"No, but—"

"Then there's no problem."

"I don't usually go out for dinner, Mr. Kling, unless someone is escorting me."

"I'll be escorting you."

"That's not what I meant. I'm a working girl. I can't afford—"

"Well, I'm sorry about the financial agreements, but as I explained—"

"Yes, well, you just tell your lieutenant I can't afford a long, leisurely dinner every night, that's all. I earn a hundred and two dollars a week after taxes, Mr. Kling. I pay my own college tuition and the rent on my own apartment—"

"Well, this shouldn't take too long. If our man spots us, he may make his play fairly soon. In the meantime, we'll just have to go along with it. Have you seen the new Hitchcock movie?"

"What?"

"The new—"

"No, I haven't."

"I thought we'd go see it after dinner."

"Why?"

"Got to stay together." Kling paused. "I could suggest a long walk as an alternative, but it might be pretty chilly by tonight."

"I could suggest your going directly home after dinner," Cindy said. "As an alternative, you understand. Because to tell the truth, Mr. Kling, I'm pretty damned tired by the end of a working day. In fact, on Tuesdays, Wednesdays, and Thursdays, I barely have time to grab a hamburger before I run over to the school. I'm not a rah-rah party girl. I think you ought to understand that."

"Lieutenant's orders," Kling said.

"Yeah, well, tell *him* to go see the new Hitchcock movie. I'll have dinner with you, if you insist, but right after that I'm going to bed." Cindy paused. "And I'm *not* suggesting that as an alternative."

"I didn't think you were."

"Just so we know where we stand."

"I know exactly where we stand," Kling said. "There are a lot of people in this city, Miss Forrest, and one of them is the guy who's after you. I don't know how long it'll take to smoke him out, I don't know when or where he'll spot us. But I *do* know he's not going to see us together if you're safe and cozy in your little bed and I'm safe and cozy in mine." Kling took a deep breath. "So what we're going to do, Miss Forrest, is have dinner together tonight, and then see the Hitchcock movie. And then we'll go for coffee and something afterwards, and then I'll take you home. Tomorrow's Saturday, so we can plan on a nice long day together. Sunday, too. On Monday—"

"Oh, God," Cindy said.

"You said it," Kling answered. "Cheer up, here comes your lasagna."

Because a white man punched a Negro in a bar on Culver Avenue just about the time Cindy Forrest was putting her first forkful of lasagna into her mouth, five detectives of the 87th Precinct were pressed into emergency duty to quell what looked like the beginnings of a full-scale riot. Two of those detectives were Meyer and Carella, the theory being that Stan Gifford was already dead and gone whereas the Culver Avenue fist fight could possibly lead to a good many more corpses before nightfall if something were not done about it immediately.

There was, of course, nothing that could be done about it immediately. A riot will either start or not start, and all too often the presence of policemen will only help to inflame a gathering crowd, defeating the reason of their being there in the first place. The patrolmen and detectives of the 87th could only play a waiting game, calming citizens wherever they could, spotting people they knew in the crowd and talking good sense to them, assuring them that *both* men involved in the fight had been arrested, and not only the Negro. There were some who could be placated, and others who would not. The cops roamed the streets like instant father images, trying to bind the wounds of a century by speaking belated words of peace, by patting a shoulder tolerantly, by asking to be accepted as friends. Too many of the cops were not friends and the people knew goddamn well they weren't. Too many of the cops were angry men with angry notions of their own about Negroes and Puerto Ricans, inborn prejudices that neither example nor reprimand could change. It was touch and go for a long while on that windy October afternoon.

By four o'clock, the crowds began to disperse. The patrolmen were left behind in double strength, but the detectives were relieved to resume their investigations. Meyer and Carella went downtown to see Maria Vallejo.

Her street was in one of the city's better neighborhoods, a block of old brownstones with clean-swept stoops and curtained front doors. They entered the tiny lobby with its polished brass mailboxes and bell buttons, found a listing for Maria in apartment twenty-two, and rang the bell. The answering buzz was long and insistent; it continued noisily behind them as they climbed the carpeted steps to the second floor. They rang the bell outside the door with its polished brass 2s. It opened almost immediately.

Maria was small and dark and bursting with energy. She was perhaps thirty-two, with thick black hair pulled tightly to the back of her head, flashing brown eyes, a generous mouth, and a nose that had been turned up by a plastic surgeon. She wore a white blouse and black tapered slacks. A pair of large gold hoop earrings adorned her ears, but she wore no other jewelry. She opened the door as though she were expecting party guests and then looked out at the detectives in undisguised puzzlement.

"Yes?" she said. "What is it?" She spoke without a trace of accent. If Carella had been forced to make a regional guess based on her speech, he'd have chosen Boston or one of its suburbs.

"We're from the police," he said, flashing his buzzer. "We're investigating the death of Stan Gifford."

"Oh, sure," she said. "Come on in."

They followed her into the apartment. The apartment was furnished in brimming good taste, cluttered with objects picked up in the city's better antique and junk shops. The shelves and walls were covered with ancient nutcrackers and old theater posters and a French puppet, and watercolor sketches for costumes and stage sets, and several enameled army medals, and a black silk fan, and pieces of driftwood. The living room was small, with wide curtained windows overlooking the street, luminous with the glow of the afternoon sun. It was furnished with a sofa and chair covered in deep-green velvet, a bentwood rocker, a low needle-point footstool, a marble-topped table on which lay several copies of *Paris Match*.

"Do sit down," Maria said. "Can I get you a drink? Oh, you're not allowed, are you? Some coffee?"

"I can use a cup," Carella said.

"It's on the stove. I'll just pour it. I always keep a pot on the stove. I guess I drink a million cups of coffee a day." She went into the small kitchen. They could see her standing at a round, glass-topped table over which hung a Tiffany lampshade, pouring the coffee from an enameled, hand-painted pot. She carried the cups, spoons, sugar, and cream into the living room on a small teakwood tray, shoved aside the copies of the French magazine to make room for it, and then served the detectives. She went to sit in the bentwood rocker then, sipping at her coffee, rocking idly back and forth.

"I bought this when Kennedy was killed," she said. "Do you like it? It keeps falling apart. What did you want to know about Stan?"

"We understand you were in his dressing room with him Wednesday night just before he went on, Miss Vallejo. Is that right?"

"That's right," she said.

"Were you alone with him?"

"No, there were several people in the room."

"Who?"

"Gee, I don't remember offhand. I think Art was there, yes . . . and maybe one other person."

"George Cooper?"

"Yes, that's right. Say, how did *you* know?"

Carella smiled. "But Mr. Cooper didn't come into the room, did he?"

"Oh, sure he did."

"What I mean is, he simply knocked on the door and called Mr. Gifford, isn't that right?"

"No, he came in," Maria said. "He was there quite a while."

"How much time would you say Mr. Cooper spent in the dressing room?"

"Oh, maybe five minutes."

"You remember that clearly, do you?"

"Oh, yes. He was there, all right."

"What else do you remember, Miss Vallejo? What happened in that dressing room Wednesday night?"

"Oh, nothing. We were just talking. Stan was relaxing while those singers were on, and I just sort of drifted in to have a smoke and chat, that's all."

"What did you chat about?"

"I don't remember." She shrugged. "It was just small talk. The monitor was going and those nuts were singing in the background, so we were just making small talk, that's all."

"Did Mr. Gifford eat anything? Or drink anything?"

"Gee, no. No, he didn't. We were just talking."

"No coffee? Nothing like that?"

"No. No, I'm sorry."

"Did he take a vitamin pill? Would you happen to have noticed that?"

"Gee, no, I didn't notice."

"Or *any* kind of a pill?"

"No, we were just talking, that's all."

"Did you like Mr. Gifford?"

"Well . . ."

Maria hesitated. She got out of the rocker and walked to a coffee table near the couch. She put down her cup, and then walked back to the rocker again, and then shrugged.

"Did you like him, Miss Vallejo?"

"I don't like to talk about the dead," she said.

"We were talking about him just fine until a minute ago."

"I don't like to speak *ill* of the dead," she corrected.

"Then you didn't like him?"

"Well, he was a little demanding, that's all."

"Demanding how?"

"I'm the show's wardrobe mistress, you know."

"Yes, we know."

"I've got eight people working under me. That's a big staff. I'm responsible for all of them, and it's not easy to costume that show each week, believe me. Well, I . . . I don't think Stan made the job any easier, that's all. He . . . well . . . well, really, he didn't *know* very much about costumes, and he pretended he did, and . . . well, he got on my nerves sometimes, that's all."

"I see," Carella said.

"But you went into his dressing room to chat, anyway," Meyer said through his nose, and then sniffed.

"Well, there wasn't a feud between us or anything like that. It's just that every once in a while, we yelled at each other a little, that's all. Because he didn't know a damn thing about costumes, and I happen to know a great deal about costumes, that's all. But that didn't stop me from going into his dressing room to chat a little. I don't see anything so terribly wrong about going into his dressing room to chat a little.''

"No one said anything was wrong, Miss Vallejo."

"I mean, I know a man's been murdered and all, but that's no reason to start examining every tiny little word that was said, or every little thing that was done. People *do* argue, you know.''

"Yes, we know."

Maria paused. She stopped rocking, and she turned her head toward the curtained windows streaming sunlight and very softly said, "Oh, what's the use? I guess they've already told you Stan and I hated each other's guts." She shrugged her shoulders hopelessly. "I think he was going to fire me. I heard he wouldn't put up with me any longer.''

"Who told you that?"

"David. He said—David Krantz, our producer—he said Stan was about to give me the ax. That's why I went to his dressing room Wednesday night. To ask him about it, to try to . . . well, the job pays well. Personalities shouldn't enter into a person's work. I didn't want to lose the job, that's all.''

"*Did* you discuss the job with him?"

"I started to, but then Art came in, and right after that George, so I didn't get a chance." She paused again. "I guess it's academic now, isn't it?"

"I guess so."

Meyer blew his nose noisily, put his tissue away, and then casually said, "Are you very well known in the field, Miss Vallejo?"

"Oh, yes, sure."

"So even if Mr. Gifford *had* fired you, you could always get another job. Isn't that so?"

"Well . . . word gets around pretty fast in this business. It's not good to get fired from *any* job, I'm sure you know that. And in television . . . I would have preferred to resign, that's all. So I wanted to clear it up, you see, which is why I went to his dressing room. To clear it up. If it was true he was going to let me go, I wanted the opportunity of leaving the job of my own volition, that's all.''

"But you never got a chance to discuss it."

"No. I told you. Art walked in."

"Well, thank you, Miss Vallejo," Carella said, rising. "That was very good coffee."

"Listen . . ."

She had come out of the bentwood rocker now, the rocker still moving back and forth, and she stood in the center of the room with the sun blazing on the curtains behind her. She worried her lip for a moment, and then said, "Listen, I didn't have anything to do with this."

Meyer and Carella said nothing.

"I didn't like Stan, and maybe he was going to fire me, but I'm not nuts, you know. I'm a little temperamental maybe, but I'm not nuts. We didn't get along, that's all. That's no reason to kill a man. I mean, a lot of people on the show didn't get along with Stan. He was a difficult man, that's all, and the star. We blew our stacks every now and then, that's all. But I didn't kill him. I . . . I wouldn't know how to begin hurting someone."

The detectives kept staring at her. Maria gave a small shrug.

"That's all," she said.

The afternoon was dying by the time they reached the street again. Carella glanced at his watch and said, "Let's call Bob, see if he had any luck with our friend Wetherley."

"You call," Meyer said. "I feel miserable."

"You'd better get to bed," Carella said.

"You know what Fanny Brice said is the best cure for a cold, don't you?" Meyer asked.

"No, what?"

"Put a hot Jew on your chest."

"Better take some aspirin, too," Carella advised.

They went into the nearest drugstore, and Carella called the squadroom. O'Brien told him he had tried Wetherley's number three times that afternoon, but no one had answered the phone. Carella thanked him, hung up, and went out to the car, where Meyer was blowing his nose and looking very sick indeed. By the time they got back to the squadroom, O'Brien had called the number a fourth time, again without luck. Carella told Meyer to get the hell home, but Meyer insisted on typing up at least one of the reports on the people they'd talked to in the past two days. He left the squadroom some twenty minutes before Carella. Carella finished the reports in time to greet his relief, Andy Parker, who was a half hour late as usual. He tried Wetherley's number once more, and then told Parker to keep trying it all night long, and to call him at home if he reached Wetherley. Parker assured him that he would, but Carella wasn't at all sure he'd keep the promise.

He got home to his house in Riverhead at seven-fifteen. The twins met him at the door, almost knocking him over in their headlong rush to greet him. He picked up one under each arm, and was swinging them toward the kitchen when the telephone rang.

He put down the children and went to the phone.

"Hello?" he said.

"Bet you thought I wouldn't, huh?" the voice said.

"Who's this?"

"Andy Parker. I just called Wetherley. He told me he got home about ten minutes ago. I advised him to stick around until you got there."

"Oh," Carella said. "Thanks."

He hung up and turned toward the kitchen, where Teddy was standing in the doorway. He looked at her silently for several moments, and she stared back at him, and then he shrugged and said simply, "I guess I can eat before I leave."

Teddy sighed almost imperceptibly, but Mark, the elder of the twins by five minutes, was watching the byplay with curious intensity. He made a vaguely resigned gesture with one hand and said, "There he goes." And April, thinking it was a game, threw herself into Carella's arms, squeezed the breath out of him, and squealed, "There he goes, there he goes, there he goes!"

Art Wetherley was waiting for him when he got there. He led Carella through the apartment and into a studio

overlooking the park. The studio contained a desk on
which sat a typewriter, an ash tray, a ream of blank paper
and what looked like another ream of typewritten sheets
covered with penciled hen scratches. There were several
industry award plaques on the wall, and a low bookcase
beneath them. Wetherley gestured to one of the two chairs
in the room, and Carella sat in it. He seemed extremely
calm, eminently at ease, but the ash tray on his desk was
full of cigarettes, and he lighted another one now.

"I'm not used to getting phone calls from the police,"
he said at once.

"Well, we were here—"

"Especially when they tell me to stay where I am, not
to leave the apartment."

"Andy Parker isn't the most tactful—"

"I mean, I didn't know this was a dictatorship,"
Wetherley said.

"It isn't, Mr. Wetherley," Carella said gently. "We're
investigating a murder, however, and we were here yesterday, but—"

"I was staying with a friend."

"What friend?"

"A girl I know. I felt pretty shook up Wednesday night
after this . . . thing happened, so I went over to her
apartment. I've been there the past two days." Wetherley
paused. "There's no law against that, is there?"

"Certainly not." Carella smiled. "I'm sorry if we
inconvenienced you, but we did want to ask you some
questions."

Wetherley seemed slightly mollified. "Well, all right,"
he said. "But there was no need, really, to warn me not to
leave the apartment."

"I apologize for that, Mr. Wetherley."

"Well, all right," Wetherley said.

"I wonder if you could tell me what happened in Stan
Gifford's dressing room Wednesday night. Just before he
left it."

"I don't remember in detail."

"Well, tell me what you *do* remember."

Wetherley thought for a moment, crushed out his cigarette, lighted a new one, and then said, "Maria was there when I came in. She was arguing with Stan about something. At least . . ."

"Arguing?"

"Yes. I could hear them shouting at each other before I knocked on the door."

"Go ahead."

"The atmosphere was a little strained after I went in, and Maria didn't say very much all the while I was there. But Stan and I were joking, mostly about the folk singers. He hated folk singers, but this particular group is hot right now, and he was talked into hiring them."

"So you were making jokes about them?"

"Yes. While we watched the act on the monitor."

"I see. In a friendly manner, would you say?"

"Oh, yes."

"Then what happened?"

"Well . . . Then George came in. George Cooper, the show's a.d."

"He came into the room?"

"Yes."

"How long did he stay?"

"Oh, three or four minutes, I guess."

"I see. But *he* didn't argue with Gifford, did he?"

"No."

"Just Maria?"

"Yes. Before I got there, you understand."

"Yes, I understand. And what about you?" Carella asked.

"Me?"

"Yes. What about your argument with Gifford before the show went on the air?"

"Argument? Who said there was an argument?"

"Wasn't there one?"

"Certainly not."

Carella took a deep breath. "Mr. Wetherley, didn't you say you wished Stan Gifford would drop dead?"

"No, sir."

"You did *not* say that?"

"No, sir, I did not. Stan and I got along very well."

Wetherley paused. "A lot of people on the show *didn't* get along with him, you understand. But I never had any trouble."

"*Who* didn't get along with him, Mr. Wetherley?"

"Well, Maria, for one. I just told you that. And David Krantz didn't particularly like him. He was always saying, within earshot of Stan, that all actors are cattle, and that comedians are only funny actors. And George Cooper didn't exactly enjoy his role of . . . well, handyman, almost. Keeping everyone quiet on the set, and running for coffee, and bringing Stan his pills, and making sure everybody—"

"Bringing Stan his *what?*"

"His pills," Wetherley said. "Stan was a nervous guy, you know. I guess he was on tranquilizers. Anyway, George was the chief errand boy and bottle washer, hopping whenever Stan snapped his fingers."

"Did George bring him a pill Wednesday night?"

"When?" Wetherley asked.

"Wednesday night. When he came to the dressing room."

Wetherley concentrated for a moment, and then said, "Now that you mention it, I think he did."

"You're sure about that?"

"Yes, sir. I'm positive."

"And did Stan *take* the pill from him?"

"Yes, sir."

"And did he swallow it?"

"Yes, sir."

Carella rose suddenly. "Would you mind coming along with me, Mr. Wetherley?" he asked.

"Come along? Where?"

"Uptown. There are a few things we'd like to get straight."

The few things Carella wanted to get straight were the conflicting stories of the last three people to have been with Gifford before he went on camera. He figured that the best way to do this was in the squadroom, where the police would have the psychological advantage in the question-and-answer game. There was nothing terribly sinister about the green globes hanging outside the station house, or about the high desk in the muster room or the sign advising all visitors to stop at the desk, or even the white sign announcing DETECTIVE DIVISION in bold black letters, and pointing toward the iron-runged steps leading upstairs. There was certainly nothing menacing about the steps themselves or the narrow corridor they opened onto, or the various rooms in that corridor with their neatly lettered signs, INTERROGATION, LAVATORY, CLERICAL. The slatted-wood railing that divided the corridor from the squadroom was innocuous-looking, and the squadroom itself—in spite of the wire-mesh grads over the windows—looked like any business office in the city, with desks, and filing cabinets, and ringing telephones, and a water cooler, and bulletin boards, and men working in shirt sleeves. But Art Wetherley, Maria Vallejo, and George Cooper were visibly rattled by their surroundings, and they became more rattled when they were taken into separate rooms for their interrogations. Bob O'Brien, a big cop with a sweet and innocently boyish look, questioned Cooper in the lieutenant's office. Steve Carella questioned Maria in the Clerical Office, kicking out Alf Miscolo, who was busy typing up his records and complained bitterly. Meyer Meyer, suffering from a cold, and not ready to take any nonsense, questioned Art Wetherley at the table in the barely furnished Interrogation Room. The three detectives had decided beforehand what questions they would ask, and what their approach would be. In separate rooms, with different suspects, they went through a familiar routine.

"You said you weren't drinking coffee, Miss Vallejo," Carella said. "Mr. Cooper tells us there were coffee containers in that room. Were there or weren't there?"

"No. I don't remember. I know *I* didn't have any coffee."

"Did Art Wetherley?"

"No. I didn't see him drink anything."

"Did George Cooper hand Gifford a pill?"

"No."

"Were you arguing with Gifford before Art Wetherley came in?"

"No."

* * *

"Let's go over this one more time, Mr. Cooper," O'Brien
said. "You say you only knocked on the door and poked
your head into the room, is that right?"

"That's right."

"You were there only a few seconds."

"Yes. Look, I—"

"Did you give Stan Gifford a pill?"

"A pill? No! No, I didn't!"

"But there were coffee containers in the room, huh?"

"Yes. Look, I didn't give him anything! What are you
trying . . . ?"

"Did you hear Art Wetherley say he wished Gifford
would drop dead?"

"Yes!"

"All right, Wetherley," Meyer said, "when did Cooper
give him that pill?"

"As soon as he came into the room."

"And Gifford washed it down with what?"

"With the coffee we were drinking."

"You were all drinking coffee, huh?"

"Yes."

"*Who* was?"

"Maria, and Stan, and I was, too."

"Then why'd you go to that room, Maria, if not to
argue?"

"I went to . . . to talk to him. I thought we could—"

"But you *were* arguing, weren't you?"

"No. I swear to God, I wasn't—"

"Then why are you lying about the coffee? Were you
drinking coffee, or weren't you?"

"No. No coffee. Please, I . . ."

"Now hold it, hold it, Mr. Cooper. You were either in
that room or not in it. You either gave him a pill or
you—"

"I didn't, I'm telling you."

"Did you *ever* give him pills?"

"No."

"He was taking tranquilizers, wasn't he?"

"I don't know what he was taking. I never brought him anything."

"Never?"

"Once maybe, or twice. An aspirin. If he had a headache."

"But never a tranquilizer?"

"No."

"How about a vitamin capsule?"

"He handed him the pill," Wetherley said.

"What kind of a pill?"

"I don't know."

"Think!"

"I'm thinking. A small pill."

"What color?"

"White."

"A tablet, you mean? Like an aspirin? Like that?"

"Yes. Yes, I think so. I don't remember."

"Well, you saw it, didn't you?"

"Yes, but . . ."

They put it all together afterward in the squadroom. They left the three suspects in the lieutenant's office with a patrolman watching over them and sat around Carella's desk and compared their answers. They were not particularly pleased with the results, but neither were they surprised by them. They had all been cops for a good many years, and nothing human beings perpetrated against each other ever surprised them. They were perhaps a little saddened by what they discovered each and every time, but never surprised. They were used to dealing with facts, and they accepted the facts in the Stan Gifford case with grim resolution.

The facts were simple and disappointing.

They decided after comparing results that all three of their suspects were lying.

Maria Vallejo *had* been arguing with Gifford, and she *had* been drinking coffee, but she denied both allegations because she realized how incriminating these seemingly isolated circumstances might seem. She recognized quite correctly that someone could have poisoned Gifford by dropping something into his coffee. If she admitted there had been coffee in the dressing room, that indeed she and Gifford had been drinking coffee together, and if she then further admitted they'd been arguing, could she not have been the one who slipped the lethal dose into the sponsor's brew? So Maria had lied in her teeth, but had graciously refused to incriminate anyone else while she was lying. It was enough for her to fabricate her own way out of what seemed like a horrible trap.

Art Wetherley had indeed wished his employer would drop dead, and he had wished it out loud, and he had wished it in the presence of someone else. And that night, lo and behold, Stan Gifford *did* collapse, on camera, for millions to see. Art Wetherley, like a child who'd made a fervent wish, was startled to realize it had come true. Not only was he startled; he was frightened. He immediately remembered what he'd said to George Cooper before the show, and he was certain Cooper would remember it, too. His fear reached new dimensions when he recalled that he had been one of the last few people to spend time with Gifford while he was alive, and that his proximity to Gifford in an obvious poisoning case, coupled with his chance remark during rehearsal, could easily serve to pin a thoroughly specious murder rap on him. When a detective called and warned him not to leave the apartment, Wetherley was certain he'd been picked as the patsy of the year, an award that did not come gold-plated like an Emmy. In desperation, he had tried to discredit Cooper's statement by turning the tables and presenting Cooper as a suspect himself. He had seen Cooper bringing aspirins to Gifford at least a few times in the past few years. He decided to elaborate on what he'd seen, inventing a pill that had never changed hands on the night Gifford died, senselessly incriminating Cooper. But a frightened man doesn't care who takes the blame, so long as it's not himself.

In much the same way, Cooper came to the sudden realization that not only was he one of the last people to be with Gifford, he was *the* last person. Even though he had spent several minutes with Gifford in the dressing room, he thought it was safer to say he had only poked his head into it. And whereas Gifford hadn't stopped to talk to a soul before he went on camera, Cooper thought it was wiser to add a mystery cameraman. Then, to clinch his own escape from what seemed like a definitely compromising position, he remembered Wetherley's earlier outburst and promptly paraded it before the investigating cops, even though he knew the expression was one that was uttered a hundred times a day during any television rehearsal.

Liars all.

But murderers none.

The detectives were convinced, after a grueling three-hour session, that these assorted liars were now babbling all in the cleansing catharsis of truth. Yes, we lied, they all separately admitted, but now we speak the truth, the shining truth. We did not kill Stan Gifford. We wouldn't know strohoosis from a hole in the wall. Besides, we are kind gentle people; look at us. Liars, yes, but murderers, no. We did not kill. That is the truth.

We did not kill.

The detectives believed them.

They had heard enough lies in their professional lives to know that truth has a shattering ring that can topple skyscrapers. They sent the three home without apologizing for any inconvenience. Bob O'Brien yawned, stretched, asked Carella if he needed him any more, put on his hat, and left. Meyer and Carella sat in the lonely squadroom and faced each other across the desk. It was five minutes to midnight. When the telephone rang, it momentarily startled them. Meyer lifted it from the cradle.

"Meyer, 87th Squad," he said. "Oh, hi, George." To Carella, he whispered, "It's Temple. I had him out checking Krantz's alibi." Into the phone again, he said, "What'd you get? Right. Uh-huh. Right. Okay, thanks." He hung up. "He finally got to the last person on Krantz's list, that Hollywood director. He'd been to the theater, just got back to the hotel. His little bimbo was with him.'' Meyer wiggled his eyebrows.

Carella looked at him wearily. "What'd Temple get?"

"He says they all confirmed Krantz's story. He got to the sponsor's booth a good fifteen minutes before the show went on, and he was there right up to the time Gifford got sick."

"Mmm," Carella said.

They stared at each other glumly. Midnight had come and gone; it was another day. Meyer sniffed noisily. Carella yawned and then washed his hand over his face.

"What do you think?" he said.

"I don't know. What do *you* think?"

"I don't know."

The men were silent.

"Maybe he *did* kill himself," Carella said.

"Maybe."

"Oh, man, I'm exhausted," Carella said.

Meyer sniffed.

6

He had followed them to the restaurant and the movie theater, and now he stood in the doorway across from her house, waiting for her to come home. It was a cold night, and he stood huddled deep in the shadows, his coat collar pulled high on the back of his neck, his hands thrust into his coat pockets, his hat low on his forehead.

It was ten minutes past twelve, and they had left the movie theater at eleven-forty-five, but he knew they would be coming straight home. He had been watching the girl long enough now to know a few things about her, and one of those things was that she didn't sleep around much. Last month sometime, she had shacked up with a guy on Banning Street, just for the night, and the next morning after she left the apartment he had gone up to the guy and had worked him over with a pair of brass knuckles, leaving him crying like a baby on the kitchen floor. He had warned the guy against calling the police, and he had also told him he should never go near Cindy Forrest again, never try to see her again, never even try to call her again. The guy had held his broken mouth together with one bloody hand, and nodded his head, and begged not to be hit again—that was one guy who wouldn't be bothering *her* any more. So he knew she didn't sleep around too much, and besides he knew she wouldn't be going any place but straight home with this blond guy because this blond guy was a cop.

He had got the fuzz smell from him almost the minute he first saw him, early this afternoon when he came to the office to take her to lunch. He knew the look of fuzz and the smell of fuzz, and he realized right off that the very smart bulls of this wonderful city were setting a trap for him, and that he was supposed to fall right into it—here I am, fuzz, take me.

Like fun.

He had stayed far away from the restaurant where they had lunch, getting the fuzz stink sharp and clear in his nostrils and knowing something was up, but not knowing what kind of a trap was being set for him, and wanting to make damn sure before he made another move. The blond guy walked like a cop, that was an unmistakable cop walk. And also he had a sneaky way of making the scene, his head turned in one direction while he was really casing the opposite direction, a very nice fuzz trick that known criminals sometimes utilized, but that mostly cops from here to Detroit and back again were very familiar with. Well, he had known cops all across this fine little country of America, he had busted more cops' heads than he could count on all his fingers and toes. He wouldn't mind busting another, just for the fun of it, but not until he knew what the trap was. The one thing he wasn't going to do was walk into no trap.

In the wintertime, or like now when it was getting kind of chilly and a guy had to wear a coat, you could always tell when he was heeled because if he was wearing a shoulder harness, the button between the top one and the third one was always left unbuttoned. If he was wearing the holster clipped to his belt, then a button was left undone just above the waist, so the right hand could reach in and draw—that was the first concrete tipoff that Blondie was a cop. He was a cop, and he wore his gun clipped to his belt. Watching him from outside the plate-glass window of the second restaurant later that day, there had been the flash of Blondie's tin when he went to pay his check, opening his wallet, with the shield catching light for just a second. That was the second concrete fact, and a smart man don't need more than one or two facts to piece together a story, not when the fuzz smell is all over the place to begin with.

The only thing he didn't know now was what the trap was, and whether or not he should accommodate Blondie by walking into it and maybe beating him up. He thought it would be better to work on the girl, though. It was time the girl learned what she could do and couldn't do, there was no sense putting it off. The girl had to know that she couldn't go sleeping around with no guys on Banning Street, or for that matter any place in the city. And she also had to know she couldn't play along with the cops on whatever trap they were cooking up. She had to know it now, and once and for all, because he wasn't planning on staying in the shadows for long. The girl had to know she was *his* meat and his *alone*.

He guessed he'd beat her up tonight.

He looked at his watch again. It was fifteen minutes past twelve, and he began to wonder what was keeping them. Maybe he should have stuck with them when they came out of the movie house, instead of rushing right over here. Still, if Blondie—

A car was turning into the street.

He pulled back into the shadows and waited. The car came up the street slowly. Come on, Blondie, he thought, you ain't being followed, there's no reason to drive so slow. He grinned in the darkness. The car pulled to the curb. Blondie got out and walked around to the other side, holding open the door for the girl, and then walking her up the front steps. The building was a grey, four-story job, and the girl lived on the top floor rear. The name on the bell read C. FORREST, that was the first thing he'd found out about her, almost two months ago. A little while after that, he'd broken open the lock on her mailbox and found two letters addressed to Miss Cynthia Forrest—it was a good thing she wasn't married, because if she was, her husband would have been in for one hell of a time—and another letter addressed to Miss Cindy Forrest, this one from a guy over in Thailand, serving with the Peace Corps. The guy was lucky he was over in Thailand, or he'd have had a

visitor requesting him to stop writing letters to little
Sweetpants.

Blondie was unlocking the inner vestibule door for her
now. The girl said good night—he could hear her voice
clear across the street—and Blondie gave her the keys and
said something with his back turned, and which couldn't
be heard. Then the door closed behind her, and Blondie
came down the steps, walking with a funny fuzz walk, like
a boxer moving toward the ring where a pushover sparring
partner was waiting, and keeping his head ducked, though
this was a cop trick and those eyes were most likely
flashing up and down the street in either direction even
though the head was ducked and didn't seem to be turning.
Blondie got into the car—the engine was still running—put
it into gear, and drove off.

He waited.

In five minutes' time, the car pulled around the corner
again and drifted slowly past the grey building.

He almost burst out laughing. What did Blondie think
he was playing around with, an amateur? He waited until
the car rounded the corner again, and then he waited for at
least another fifteen minutes, until he was sure Blondie
wasn't coming back.

He crossed the street rapidly then, and walked around
the corner and into the building directly behind the girl's.
He went straight through the building, opening the door at
the rear of the ground floor and stepping out into the back
yard. He climbed the clothesline pole near the fence sepa-
rating the yard from the one behind it, leaped over the
fence, and dropped to his knees. Looking up, he could see
a light burning in the girl's window on the fourth floor. He
walked toward the rear of the building, cautiously but
easily, jumping up for the fire-escape ladder, pulling it
down, and then swinging up onto it and beginning to
climb. He went by each window with great care, especially the other lighted one on the second floor, flitting
past it like a shadow and continuing on up to the third
floor, and then stepping onto the fourth-floor fire escape,
her fire escape.

There was a wooden cheese box resting on the iron slats

of the fire-escape floor, the dried twigs of dead flowers stuck into the stiff earth it contained. The fire escape was outside her bedroom. He peered around the edge of the window, but the room was empty. He glanced to his right and saw that the tiny bathroom window was lighted; the girl was in the bathroom. He debated going right into the bedroom while she was occupied down the hall, but decided against it. He wanted to wait until she was in bed. He wanted to scare her real good.

The only light in the room came from a lamp on the night table near the girl's bed. The bed was clearly visible from where he crouched outside on the fire escape. There was a single chair on this side of the bed, he would have to avoid that in the dark. He wanted his surprise to be complete; he didn't want to go stumbling over no furniture and waking her up before it was time. The window was open just a trifle at the top, probably to let in some air, she'd probably opened it when she came into the apartment. He didn't know whether or not she'd close and lock it before going to bed, maybe she would. This was a pretty decent neighborhood, though, without any incidents lately— he'd checked on that because he was afraid some cheap punk might bust into the girl's apartment and complicate things for him—so maybe she slept with the window open just a little, at the top, the way it was now. While she was in the bathroom, he studied the simple lock on the sash and decided it wouldn't be a problem, anyway, even if she locked it.

The bathroom light went out suddenly.

He flattened himself against the brick wall of the building. The girl was humming when she came into the room. The humming trailed off abruptly, she was turning on the radio. It came on very loud, for Christ's sake, she was going to wake up the whole damn building! She kept twisting the dial until she found the station she wanted, sweet music, lots of violins and muted trumpets, and then she lowered the volume. He waited. In a moment, she came to the window and pulled down the shade. Good, he thought, she didn't lock the window. He waited a moment longer, and then flattened himself onto the fire escape so

that he could peer into the room beneath the lower edge of
the shade, where the girl had left a good two-inch gap
between it and the window sill.

The girl was still dressed. She was wearing the tan dress
she had worn to dinner with Blondie, but when she turned
away and began walking toward the closet, he saw that she
had already lowered the zipper at the back. The dress was
spread in a wide V, the white elastic line of her brassiere
crossing her back, the zipper lowered to a point just above
the beginning curve of her buttocks. The radio was playing
a song she knew, and she began humming along with it
again as she opened the closet door and took her nightgown from a hook. She closed the door and then walked to
the bed, sitting on the side facing the window and lifting
her dress up over her thighs to unhook first one garter and
then the other. She took off her shoes and rolled down her
stockings, and then walked to the closet to put the shoes
away and to put the stockings into some kind of a bag
hanging on the inside doorknob. She closed the door again,
and then took off her dress, standing just outside the closet
and not moving toward the bed again. In her bra and half
slip, she walked over to the other side of the room, where
he couldn't see her any more, almost as if the lousy little
bitch knew he was watching her! She was still humming.
His hands were wet. He dried them on the sleeves of his
coat and waited.

She came back so suddenly that she startled him. She
had taken off her underwear, and she walked swiftly to the
bed, naked, to pick up her nightgown. Jesus, she was
beautiful! Jesus, he hadn't realized how goddamn beautiful
she really was. He watched her as she bent slightly to pull
the gown over her head, straightened, and then let it fall
down over her breasts and her tilted hips. She yawned.
She looked at her watch and then went across the room
again, out of sight, and came back to the bed carrying a
paperback book. She got into the bed, her legs parting,
opening, as she swung up onto it, and then pulled the
blanket up over her knees, and fluffed the pillow, and
scratched her jaw, and opened the book. She yawned. She
looked at her watch again, seemed to change her mind

about reading the book, put it down on the night table, and yawned again.

A moment later, she turned out the light.

The first thing she heard was the voice.

It said "Cindy," and for the briefest tick of time she thought she was dreaming because the voice was just a whisper. And then she heard it again, "Cindy," hovering somewhere just above her face, and her eyes popped wide, and she tried to sit up but something pressed her fiercely back against the pillow. She opened her mouth to scream, but a hand clamped over her lips. She stared over the edge of the thick fingers into the darkness, trying to see. "Be quiet, Cindy," the voice said. "Just be quiet now."

His grip on her mouth was hard and tight. He was straddling her now, his knees on the bed, his legs tight against her pinioned arms, sitting on her abdomen, one arm flung across her chest, holding her to the pillow.

"Can you hear me?" he asked.

She nodded. His hand stayed tight on her mouth, hurting her. She wanted to bite his hand, but she could not free her mouth. His weight upon her was unbearable. She tried to move, but she was helplessly caught in the vise of his knees, the tight band of his arm thrown across her chest.

"Listen to me," he said. "I'm going to beat the shit out of you."

She believed him instantly; terror rocketed into her skull. Her eyes were growing accustomed to the darkness. She could dimly see his grinning face hovering above her. His fingers smelled of tobacco. He kept his right hand clamped over her mouth, his left arm thrown across her chest, lower now, so that the hand was gripping her breast. He kept working his hand as he talked to her, grasping her through the thin nylon gown, squeezing her nipple as his voice continued in a slow lazy monotone, "Do you know why I'm going to beat you, Cindy?"

She tried to shake her head, but his hand was so tight against her mouth that she could not move. She knew she would begin to cry within the next few moments. She was trembling beneath his weight. His hand was cruel on her breast. Each time he tightened it on her nipple, she winced with pain.

"I don't like you to go out with cops," he said. "I don't like you to go out with *anybody*, but cops especially."

She could see his face clearly now. He was the same man who had come to the office, the same man who had beaten up the policeman. She remembered the way he had kicked the policeman when he was on the floor, and she began trembling more violently. She heard him laugh.

"I'm going to take my hand off your mouth now," he said, "because we have to talk. But if you scream, I'll kill you. Do you understand me?"

She tried to nod. His hand was relaxing. He was slowly lifting it from her mouth, cupped, as though cautiously peering under it to see if he had captured a fly. She debated screaming, and knew at once that if she did he would keep his promise and kill her. He shifted his body to the left, relaxing his grip across her chest, lifting his arm, freeing her breast. He rested his hands palms downward on his thighs, his legs bent under him, his knees still holding her arms tightly against her side, most of his weight still on her abdomen. Her breast was throbbing with pain. A trickle of sweat rolled down toward her belly and she thought for a moment it was blood, had he made her bleed somehow? A new wave of fear caused her to begin trembling again. She was ashamed of herself for being so frightened, but the fear was something uncontrollable, a raw animal panic that shrieked silently of pain and possible death.

"You'll get rid of him tomorrow," he whispered. He sat straddling her with his huge hands relaxed on his own thighs.

"Who?" she said. "Who do you—"

"The cop. You'll get rid of him tomorrow."

"All right." She nodded in the darkness. "All right," she said again.

"You'll call his precinct—what precinct is it?"

"The eight . . . the 87th, I think."

"You'll call him."

"Yes. Yes, I will."

"You'll tell him you don't need a police escort no more. You'll tell him everything is all right now."

"Yes, all right," she said. "Yes, I will."

"You'll tell him you patched things up with your boy friend."

"My . . ." She paused. Her heart was beating wildly, she was sure he could feel her heart beating in panic. "My *boy* friend?"

"Me," he said, and grinned.

"I . . . I don't even know you," she said.

"I'm your boy friend."

She shook her head.

"I'm your lover."

She kept shaking her head.

"Yes."

"I don't *know* you," she said, and suddenly she began weeping. "What do you want from me? Please, won't you go? Won't you please leave me alone? I don't even know you. Please, please."

"Beg," he said, and grinned.

"Please, please, please . . ."

"You're going to tell him to stop coming around."

"Yes, I *am*. I *said* I would."

"Promise."

"I promise."

"You'll keep the promise," he said flatly.

"Yes, I will. I told you—"

He slapped her suddenly and fiercely, his right hand abruptly leaving his thigh and coming up viciously toward her face. She blinked her eyes an instant before his open palm collided with her cheek. She pulled back rigidly, her neck muscles taut, her eyes wide, her teeth clamped together.

"You'll keep the promise," he said, "because this is a sample of what you'll get if you don't."

And then he began beating her.

She did not know where she was at first. She tried to open her eyes, but something was wrong with them, she could not seem to open her eyes. Something rough was against her cheek, her head was twisted at a curious angle.

She felt a hundred separate throbbing areas of hurt, but none of them seemed connected with her head or her body, each seemed to pulse with a solitary intensity of its own. Her left eye trembled open. Light knifed into the narrow crack of opening eyelid, she could open it no further. Light flickered into the tentative opening, flashes of light pulsated as the flesh over her eye quivered.

She was lying with her cheek pressed to the rug.

She kept trying to open her left eye, catching fitful glimpses of grey carpet as the eye opened and closed spasmodically, still not knowing where she was, possessing a sure knowledge that something terrible had happened to her, but not remembering what it was as yet. She lay quite still on the floor, feeling each throbbing knot of pain, arms, legs, thighs, breasts, nose, the separate pains combining to form a recognizable mass of flesh that was her body, a whole and unified body that had been severely beaten.

And then, of course, she remembered instantly what had happened.

Her first reaction was one of whimpering terror. She drew up her shoulders, trying to pull her head deeper into them. Her left hand came limply toward her face, the fingers fluttering, as though weakly trying to fend off any further blows.

"Please," she said.

The word whispered into the room. She waited for him to strike her again, every part of her body tensed for another savage blow, and when none came, she lay trembling lest she was mistaken, fearful that he was only pretending to be gone while silently waiting to attack again.

Her eye kept flickering open and shut.

She rolled over onto her back and tried to open the other eye, but again only a crack of winking light came through the trembling lid. The ceiling seemed so very far away. Sobbing, she brought her hand to her nose, thinking it was running, wiping it with the back of her hand, and then realizing that blood was pouring from her nostrils.

"Oh," she said. "Oh, my God."

She lay on her back, sobbing in anguish. At last, she

tried to rise. She made it to her knees, and then fell to the floor again, sprawled on her face. The police, she thought, I must call the police. And then she remembered why he had beaten her. He did not want the police. Get rid of the police, he had said. She got to her knees again. Her gown was torn down the front. Her breasts were splotched with purple bruises. The nipple of her right breast looked as raw as an open wound. Her throat, the torn gown, the sloping tops of her breasts were covered with blood from her nose. She cupped her hand under it, and then tried to stop the flow by holding a torn shred of nylon under the nostrils, struggling to her feet and moving unsteadily toward her dressing table, where she knew she'd left her house keys, Kling had returned her house keys, she had left them on the dresser, she would put them at the back of her neck, they would stop the blood, groping for the dresser top, a severe pain on the side of her chest, had he kicked her the way he'd kicked that policeman, get rid of the police, oh my God, oh God, oh God dear God.

She could not believe what she saw in the mirror.

The image that stared back at her was grotesque and frightening, hideous beyond belief. Her eyes were puffed and swollen, the pupils invisible, only a narrow slit showing on the bursting surface of each discolored bulge. Her face was covered with blood and bruises, a swollen mass of purple lumps, her blond hair was matted with blood, there were welts on her arms, and thighs, and legs.

She felt suddenly dizzy. She clutched the top of the dressing table to steady herself, taking her hand away from her nose momentarily, watching the falling drops of blood spatter onto the white surface. A wave of nausea came and passed. She stood with her hand pressed to the top of the table, leaning on her extended arm, her head bent, refusing to look into the mirror again. She must not call the police. If she called the police, he would come back and do this to her again. He had told her to get rid of the police, she would call Kling in the morning and tell him everything was all right now, she and her boy friend had patched it up. In utter helplessness, she began crying again, her shoulders heaving, her nose dripping blood, her knees shaking as she clung to the dressing table for support.

Gasping for breath, she stood suddenly erect and opened her mouth wide, sucking in great gulps of air, her hands widespread over her belly like an open fan. Her fingers touched something wet and sticky, and she looked down sharply, expecting more blood, expecting to find herself soaked in blood that seeped from a hundred secret wounds.

She raised her hand slowly toward her swollen eyes.

She fainted when she realized the wet and sticky substance on her belly was semen.

Bert Kling kicked down the door of her apartment at ten-thirty the next morning. He had begun trying to reach her at nine, wanting to work out the details of their day together. He had let the phone ring seven times, and then decided he'd dialed the wrong number. He hung up, and tried it again. This time, he let it ring for a total of ten times, just in case she was a heavy sleeper. There was no answer. At nine-thirty, hoping she had gone down for breakfast and returned to the apartment by now, he called once again. There was still no answer. He called at five minute intervals until ten o'clock, and then clipped on his gun and went down to his car. It took him a half hour to drive from Riverhead to Cindy's apartment on Glazebrook Street. He climbed the steps to the fourth floor, knocked on her door, called her name, and then kicked it open.

He phoned for an ambulance immediately.

She regained consciousness briefly before the ambulance arrived. When she recognized him, she mumbled, "No, please, get out of here, he'll know," and then passed out again.

Outside Cindy's open bedroom window, Kling discovered a visible heel print on one of the iron slats of the fire escape, just below the sill. And very close to that, wedged between two of the slats, he found a small fragment of something that looked like wadded earth. There was the possibility, however small, that the fragment had been dislodged from the shoe of Cindy's attacker. He scooped it into a manila envelope and marked it for transportation to Detective-Lieutenant Sam Grossman at the police laboratory.

7

Every time Kling went downtown to the lab on High Street, he felt the way he had when he was eleven years old and his parents gave him a Gilbert Chemistry Set for Christmas. The lab covered almost half the first-floor area of the Headquarters building, and although Kling realized it was undoubtedly a most mundane place to Grossman and his cohorts, to him it was a wonderland of scientific marvel. To him, there was truth and justice in the orderly arrangement of cameras and filters, spotlights and enlargers, condensers and projectors. There was an aura of worlds unknown in the silent array of microscopes, common and stereoscopic, comparison and polarizing. There was magic in the quartz lamp with its ultraviolet light, there was poetry in the beakers and crucibles, the flasks and tripods, the burettes and pipettes, the test tubes and Bunsen burners. The police lab was *Mechanics Illustrated* come to life, with balance scales and drafting tools, tape measures and micrometers, scalpels and microtomes, emery wheels and vises. And hovering over it all was the aroma of a thousand chemicals, hitting the nostrils like a waft of exotic perfume caught in the single sail of an Arabian bark.

He loved it, and he wandered into it like a small boy each time, often forgetting that he had come there to discuss the facts of violence or death.

Sam Grossman never forgot the facts of violence or death. He was a tall man, big-boned, with the hands and face of a New England farmer. His eyes were blue and guileless behind thick-rimmed eyeglasses. He spoke softly and with a gentility and warmth reminiscent of an era long past, even though his voice carried the clipped stamp of a man who dealt continually with cold scientific fact. Taking off his glasses in the police lab that Monday morning, he wiped the lenses with a corner of his white lab coat, put them back on the bridge of his nose, and said, "You gave us an interesting one this time, Bert."

"How so?"

"Your man was a walking catalog. We found traces of everything but the kitchen sink in that fragment."

"Anything I can use?"

"Well, that depends. Come on back here."

The men walked the length of the lab, moving between two long white counters bearing test tubes of different chemicals, some bubbling, all reminding Kling of a Franken-stein movie.

"Here's what we were able to isolate from that frag-ment. Seven different identifiable materials, all embedded in, or clinging to, or covering the basic material, which in itself is a combination of three materials. I think you were right about him having carried it on his shoe. Any other way, he couldn't have picked up such a collection of junk."

"You think it was caught on his heel?"

"Probably wedged near the rear of the shoe, where the sole joins the heel. Impossible to tell, of course. We're just guessing. It seems likely, though, considering the garbage he managed to accumulate."

"What kind of garbage?"

"Here," Grossman said.

Each minute particle or particles of "garbage" had been isolated and mounted on separate microscope slides, all of them labeled for identification. The slides were arranged vertically in a rack on the counter top, and Grossman ticked off each one with his forefinger as he explained.

"The basic composition is made up of the materials on these first three slides, blended to form a sort of mastic to which the other elements undoubtedly clung."

"And what are those three materials?" Kling asked.

"Suet, sawdust, and blood," Grossman replied.

"Human blood?"

"No. We ran the Uhlenhuth precipitin reaction test on it. It's definitely not human."

"That's good."

"Well, yes," Grossman said, "because it gives us something to play with. Where would we be most likely to find a combination of sawdust, suet, and animal blood?"

"A butcher shop?" Kling said.

"That's our guess. And our fourth slide lends support to the possibility." Grossman tapped the slide with his finger. "It's an animal hair. We weren't certain at first because the granulation resembled that of a human hair. But the medullary index—the relation between the diameter of the medulla and the diameter of the whole hair—was zero point five. Narrower than that would have indicated it was human. It's definitely animal."

"What kind of an animal?" Kling asked.

"We can't tell for certain. Either bovine or equine. Considering the other indications, the hair probably came from an animal one would expect to find in a butcher shop, most likely a steer."

"I see," Kling said. He paused. "But . . ." He paused again. "They're *stripped* by the time they get to a butcher shop, aren't they?"

"What do you mean?"

"Well, the hide's been taken off by that time."

"So?"

"Well, you just wouldn't find a hair from a steer's hide in a butcher shop, that's all."

"I see what you mean. A slaughterhouse would be a better guess, wouldn't it?"

"Sure," Kling said. He thought for a moment. "There're some slaughterhouses here in the city, aren't there?"

"I'm not sure. I think all the slaughtering's done across the river, in the next state."

"Well, at least this gives us something to look into."

"We found a few other things as well," Grossman said.

"Like what?"

"Fish scales."

"What?"

"Fish scales, or at least a single minute particle of a fish scale."

"In a slaughterhouse?"

"It doesn't sound likely, does it?"

"No. I'm beginning to like your butcher shop idea again."

"You are, huh?"

"Sure. A combined butcher shop and fish market, why not?"

"What about the animal hair?"

"A dog maybe?" Kling suggested.

"We don't think so."

"Well, how would a guy pick up a fish scale in a slaughterhouse?"

"He didn't have to," Grossman said. "He could have picked it up wherever he went walking. He could have picked it up any place in the city."

"That narrows it down a lot," Kling said.

"You've got to visualize this as a lump composed of suet, blood—"

"Yeah, and sawdust—"

"Right, that got stuck to his shoe. And you've got to visualize him walking around and having additional little pieces of garbage picked up by this sticky wad of glopis—"

"Sticky wad of *what?*"

"Glopis. That's an old Yiddish expression."

"Glopis?"

"Glopis."

"And the animal hair was stuck to the glopis, right?"

"Right."

"And also the fish scale?"

"Right."

"And what else?"

"These aren't in any particular order, you understand. I mean, it's impossible to get a progressive sequence of where he might have been. We simply—"

"I understand," Kling said.

"Okay, we found a small dot of putty, a splinter of

creosoted wood, and some metal filings which we identified as copper.''

''Go on.''

''We also found a tiny piece of peanut.''

''Peanut,'' Kling said blankly.

''That's right. And to wrap it all up, the entire sticky
suet mess of glopis was soaked with gasoline. Your friend
stepped into a lot.''

Kling took a pen from his jacket pocket. Repeating the
items out loud, and getting confirmation from Grossman as
he went along, he jotted them into his notebook:

1- Suet
2- Sawdust
3- Blood (Animal)
4- Hair (Animal)
5- Fish Scale

6- Putty
7- Wood Splinter (creosoted)
8- Metal Filings (copper)
9- Peanut
10- Gasoline

''That's it, huh?''

''That's it,'' Grossman said.

''Thanks. You just ruined my day.''

The drawing from the police artist was waiting for Kling
when he got back to the squadroom. There were five
artists working for the department, and this particular pencil sketch had been made by Detective Victor Haldeman,
who had studied at the Art Students League in New York
and later at the Art Institute in Chicago before joining the
force. Each of the five artists, before being assigned to this
special duty, had held other jobs in the department: two
of them had been patrolmen in Isola, and the remaining
three had been detectives in Calm's Point, Riverhead, and
Majesta respectively. The Bureau of Criminal Identification was located at Headquarters on High Street, several
floors above the police lab. But the men assigned to the
artists' section of the bureau worked in a studio annex at
600 Jessup Street.

Their record was an impressive one. Working solely

from verbal descriptions supplied by witnesses who were sometimes agitated and distraught, they had in the past year been responsible for twenty-eight positive identifications and arrests. So far this year, they had made sixty-eight drawings of described suspects, from which fourteen arrests had resulted. In each case, the apprehended suspect bore a remarkable resemblance to the sketch made from his description. Detective Haldeman had talked to all of the people who had been present when Vollner's office was invaded Wednesday afternoon, listening to descriptions of face, hair, eyes, nose, mouth from Miles Vollner, Cindy Forrest, Grace Di Santo, and Ronnie Fairchild, the patrolman who was still hospitalized. The composite drawing he made took three and a half hours to complete. It was delivered to Kling in a manila envelope that Monday morning. The drawing itself was protected by a celluloid sleeve into which it had been inserted. There was no note with the drawing, and the drawing was unsigned. Kling took it out of the envelope and studied it.

Andy Parker, who was strolling past Kling's desk on his way to the toilet, stopped and looked at the drawing.

"Who's that?"

"Suspect," Kling said.

"No kidding? I thought maybe it was Cary Grant."

"You know what you ought to do, Andy?" Kling asked, not looking up at him as he put the drawing back into the manila envelope.

"What?" Parker asked.

"You should join the police force. I understand they're looking for comical cops."

"Ha!" Parker said, and went out to the toilet where he hoped to occupy himself for the next half hour with a copy of *Life* Magazine.

Forty miles away from the precinct that Monday morning, twenty-five miles outside the city limits, Detectives Meyer and Carella drove through the autumn countryside on their way to Larksview and the home of Mrs. Stan Gifford.

They had spent all day Saturday and part of Sunday questioning a goodly percentage of the 212 people who

were present in the studio loft that night. They did not consider any of them possible suspects in a murder case. As a matter of fact, they were trying hard to find something substantial upon which to hang a verdict of suicide. Their line of questioning followed a single simple direction: They wanted to know whether anyone connected with the show had, at any time before or during the show, seen Stan Gifford put anything into his mouth. The answers did nothing to substantiate a theory of suicide. Most of the people connected with the show were too busy to notice who was putting what into his mouth; some of the staff hadn't come across Gifford at all during the day; and those who *had* spent any time with him had definitely not seen anything go into his mouth. A chat with David Krantz revealed that Gifford was in the habit of forestalling dinner until after the show each Wednesday, eating a heavy lunch to carry him through the day. This completely destroyed the theory that perhaps Gifford had eaten again after meeting his wife. But it provided a new possibility for speculation, and it was this possibility that took Meyer and Carella to Larksview once more.

Meyer was miserable. His nose was stuffed, his throat was sore, his eyes were puffed and swollen. He had been taking a commercial cold preparation over the weekend, but it hadn't helped him at all. He kept blowing his nose, and then talking through it, and then blowing it again. He made a thoroughly delightful partner and companion.

Happily, the reporters and photographers had forsaken the Gifford house now that the story had been pushed off the front page and onto the pages reserved for armchair detection. Meyer and Carella drove to the small parking area, walked to the front door, and once again pulled the brass knob set into the jamb. The housekeeper opened the door, peeked out cautiously, and then said, "Oh, it's you again."

"Is Mrs. Gifford home?" Carella asked.

"I'll see," she said, and closed the door in their faces. They waited on the front stoop. The woods surrounding the house rattled their autumn colors with each fresh gust of wind. In a few moments, the housekeeper returned.

"Mrs. Gifford is having coffee in the dining room," she said. "You may join her, if you wish."

"Thank you," Carella said, and they followed her into the house. A huge winding staircase started just inside the entrance hall, thickly carpeted, swinging to the upper story of the house. French doors opened onto the living room, and through that and beyond it was a small dining room with a bay window overlooking the back yard. Melanie Gifford sat alone at the table, wearing a quilted robe over a long pink nylon nightgown, the laced edges of the gown showing where the robe ended. Her blond hair was uncombed, and hung loosely about her face. As before, she wore no makeup, but she seemed more rested now, and infinitely more at ease.

"I was just having breakfast," she said. "I'm afraid I'm a late sleeper. Won't you have something?"

Meyer took the chair opposite her, and Carella sat beside her at the table. She poured coffee for both men and then offered them the English muffins and marmalade, which they declined.

"Mrs. Gifford," Carella said, "when we were here last time, you said something about your husband's physician, Carl Nelson."

"Yes," Melanie said. "Do you take sugar?"

"Thank you." Carella spooned a teaspoonful into his coffee, and then passed the sugar bowl to Meyer. "You said you thought he'd murdered—"

"Cream?"

"Thank you—your husband. Now what made you say that, Mrs. Gifford?"

"I believed it."

"Do you still believe it?"

"No."

"Why not?"

"Because I see now that it would have been impossible. I didn't know the nature of the poison at the time."

"Its speed, do you mean?"

"Yes. Its speed."

"And you mean it would have been impossible because

Dr. Nelson was at home during the show, and not at the studio, is that right?"

"Yes."

"But what made you suspect him in the first place?"

"I tried to think of who could have had access to poison, and I thought of Carl."

"So did we," Carella said.

"I imagine you would have," Melanie answered. "These muffins are very good. Won't you have some?"

"No, thank you. But even if he did have access, Mrs. Gifford, why would he have wanted to kill your husband?"

"I have no idea."

"Didn't the two men get along?"

"You know doctors," Melanie said. "They all have God complexes." She paused, and then added, "In any universe, there can only be one God."

"And in Stan Gifford's universe, *he* was God."

Melanie sipped at her coffee and said, "If an actor hasn't got his ego, then he hasn't got anything."

"Are you saying the two egos came into conflict occasionally, Mrs. Gifford?"

"Yes."

"But not in any serious way, surely."

"I don't know what men consider serious. I know that Stan and Carl occasionally argued. So when Stan was killed, as I told you, I tried to figure out who could have got his hands on any poison, and I thought of Carl."

"That was before you knew the poison was strophanthin."

"Yes. Once I found out what the poison was, and knowing Carl was home that night, I realized—"

"But if you didn't know the poison was strophanthin, then it could have been anything, any poison, isn't that right?"

"Yes. But—"

"And you also must have known that a great many poisons can be purchased in drugstores, usually in compounds of one sort or another. Like arsenic or cyanide . . ."

"Yes, I suppose I knew that."

"But you still automatically assumed Dr. Nelson had killed your husband."

"I was in shock at the time. I didn't know what to think."

"I see," Carella said. He picked up his cup and took a long deliberate swallow. "Mrs. Gifford, you said your husband took a vitamin capsule after lunch last Wednesday."

"That's right."

"Did he have that capsule with him, or did you bring it to him when you went into the city?"

"He had it with him."

"Was he in the habit of taking vitamin capsules with him?"

"Yes," Melanie said. "He was supposed to take one after every meal. Stan was a very conscientious man. When he knew he was going into the city, he carried the vitamins with him, in a small pillbox."

"Did he take only one capsule to the city last Wednesday? Or *two?*"

"One," Melanie said.

"How do you know?"

"Because there were two on the breakfast table that morning. He swallowed one with his orange juice, and he put the other in the pillbox, and then put it in his pocket."

"And you saw him take that second capsule after lunch?"

"Yes. He took it out of the pillbox and put it on the table the moment we were seated. That's what he usually did—so he wouldn't forget to take it."

"And to your knowledge, he did not have any other capsules with him. That was the only capsule he took after leaving this house last Wednesday."

"That's right."

"Who put those capsules on the breakfast table, Mrs. Gifford?"

"My housekeeper." Melanie looked suddenly annoyed. "I'm not sure I understand all this," she said. "If he took the capsule at lunch, I don't see how it could possibly—"

"We're only trying to find out for sure whether or not there were only two capsules, Mrs. Gifford."

"I just told you."

"We'd like to be sure. We know the capsule he took at lunch couldn't possibly have killed him. But if there was a third capsule—"

"There were only two," Melanie said. "He knew he was coming home for dinner after the show, the way he did every Wednesday night. There was no need for him to carry more than—"

"More than the one he took at lunch."

"Yes."

"Mrs. Gifford, do you know whether or not your husband had any insurance on his life?"

"Yes, of course he did."

"Would you know in what amount?"

"A hundred thousand dollars."

"And the company?"

"Municipal Life."

"Who's the beneficiary, Mrs. Gifford?"

"I am," Melanie replied.

"I see," Carella said.

There was a brief silence. Melanie put down her coffee cup. Her eyes met Carella's levelly. Quietly, she said, "I'm sure you didn't mean to suggest, Detective Carella—"

"Mrs. Gifford, this is all routine—"

"—that I might have had anything to do with the death of—"

"—questioning. I don't know *who* had anything to do with your husband's death."

"*I* didn't."

"I hope not."

"Because, you see, Detective Carella, a hundred thousand dollars in insurance money would hardly come anywhere near the kind of income my husband earned as a performer. I'm sure you know that he recently signed a two-million-dollar contract with the network. And I can *assure* you he's always been more than generous to me. Or perhaps you'd like to come upstairs and take a look at the furs in my closet or the jewels on my dresser."

"I don't think that'll be necessary, Mrs. Gifford."

"I'm sure it won't. But you might also like to consider

the fact that Stan's insurance policy carried the usual suicide clause.''

''I'm not sure I follow you, Mrs. Gifford.''

''I'm saying, Detective Carella, that unless you can find a murderer—unless you can *prove* there was foul play involved in my husband's death—his insurance company will conclude he was a suicide. In which case, I'll receive only the premiums already paid in, and not a penny more.''

''I see.''

''Yes, I hope you do.''

''Would you know whether or not your husband left a will, Mrs. Gifford?'' Meyer asked.

''Yes, he did.''

''Are you also a beneficiary in his will?''

''I don't know.''

''You never discussed it with him?''

''Never. I know there's a will, but I don't know what its terms are.''

''Who *would* know, Mrs. Gifford?''

''His lawyer, I imagine.''

''And the lawyer's name?''

''Salvatore Di Palma.''

''In the city?''

''Yes.''

''You won't mind if we call him?''

''Why should I?'' Melanie paused again, and again stared at Carella. ''I don't mind telling you,'' she said, ''that you're beginning to give me a severe pain in the ass.''

''I'm sorry.''

''Does part of your 'routine questioning' involve badgering a man's widow?''

''I'm sorry, Mrs. Gifford,'' Carella said. ''We're only trying to investigate every possibility.''

''Then how about investigating the possibility that I led a full and happy life with Stan? When we met, I was working in summer stock in Pennsylvania, earning sixty dollars a week. I've had everything I ever wanted from the moment we were married, but I'd gladly give all of it—the furs, the jewels, the house, even the clothes on my back—if that'd bring Stan to life again.''

"We're only—"

"Yes, you're only investigating every possibility, I know. Be human," she said. "You're dealing with people, not ciphers."

The detectives were silent. Melanie sighed.

"Did you still want to see my housekeeper?"

"Please," Meyer said.

Melanie lifted the small bell near her right hand, and gave it a rapid shake. The housekeeper, as though alert and waiting for the tiny sound, came into the dining room immediately.

"These gentlemen would like to ask you some questions, Maureen," Melanie said. "If you don't mind, gentlemen, I'll leave you alone. I'm late for an appointment now, and I'd like to get dressed."

"Thank you for your time, Mrs. Gifford," Carella said.

"Not at all," Melanie said, and walked out of the room.

Maureen stood by the table, uncertainly picking at her apron. Meyer glanced at Carella, who nodded. Meyer cleared his throat, and said, "Maureen, on the day Mr. Gifford died, did you set the breakfast table for him?"

"For him and for Mrs. Gifford, yes, sir."

"Do you always set the table?"

"Except on Thursdays and every other Sunday, which are my days off. Yes, sir, I always set the table."

"Did you put Mr. Gifford's vitamin capsules on the table that morning?" Meyer asked.

"Yes, sir. Right alongside his plate, same as usual."

"How many vitamin capsules?"

"Two."

"Not three?"

"I said two," Maureen said.

"Was anyone in the room when you put the capsules on the table?"

"No, sir."

"Who came down to breakfast first? Mr. Gifford or Mrs. Gifford?"

"Mrs. Gifford came in just as I was leaving."

"And then Mr. Gifford?"

"Yes. I heard him come down about five minutes later."

"Do these vitamin capsules come in a jar?"

"A small bottle, sir."

"Could we see that bottle, please?"

"I keep it in the kitchen." Maureen paused. "You'll have to wait while I get it."

She went out of the room. Carella waited until he could no longer hear her footfalls, and then asked, "What are you thinking?"

"I don't know. But if Melanie Gifford was alone in the room with those two capsules, she could have switched one of them, no?"

"The one he was taking to lunch, huh?"

"Yeah."

"Only one thing wrong with that theory," Carella said.

"Yeah, I know. He had lunch seven hours before he collapsed." Meyer sighed and shook his head. "We're *still* stuck with that lousy six minutes. It's driving me nuts."

"Besides, it doesn't look as though Melanie had any reason to do in her own dear Godlike husband."

"Yeah," Meyer said. "It's just I get the feeling she's too cooperative, you know? Her and the good doctor both. So very damn helpful. He right away diagnoses poison and insists we do an autopsy. She immediately points to him as a suspect, then changes her mind when she finds out about the poison. And both of them conveniently away from the studio on the night Gifford died." Meyer nodded his head, a thoughtful expression on his face. "Maybe that six minutes is *supposed* to drive us nuts."

"How do you mean?"

"Maybe we were *supposed* to find out which poison killed him. I mean, we'd naturally do an autopsy anyway, right? And we'd find out it was strophanthin, and we'd also find out how fast strophanthin works."

"Yeah, go ahead."

"So we'd automatically rule out anybody who wasn't near Gifford before he died."

"That's almost the entire city, Meyer."

"No, you know what I mean. We'd rule out Krantz, who says he was in the sponsor's booth, and we'd rule out Melanie, who was here, and Nelson, who was at his own house."

"That still needs checking," Carella said.

"Why? Krantz said that was where he reached him after Gifford collapsed."

"That doesn't mean Nelson was there all night. I want to ask him about that. In fact, I'd like to stop at his office as soon as we get back to the city."

"Okay, but do you get my point?"

"I think so. Given a dead end to work with, knowing how much poison Gifford had swallowed, and knowing how fast it worked, we'd come to the only logical conclusion: suicide. Is that what you mean?"

"Right," Meyer said.

"Only one thing wrong with your theory, friend."

"Yeah, what?"

"The facts. It *was* strophanthin. It *does* work instantly. You can speculate all you want, but the facts remain the same."

"Facts, facts," Meyer said. "All I know—"

"Facts," Carella insisted.

"Suppose Melanie did switch that lunch capsule? We still haven't checked Gifford's will. She may be in it for a healthy chunk."

"All right, suppose she did. He'd have dropped dead on his way to the studio."

"Or suppose Krantz got to him *before* he went up to the sponsor's booth?"

"Then Gifford would have shown symptoms of poisoning before the show even went on the air."

"Arrrggh, facts," Meyer said, and Maureen came back into the room.

"I asked Mrs. Gifford if it was all right," she said. She handed the bottle of vitamin capsules to Carella. "You can do whatever you like with them."

"We'd like to take them with us, if that's all right."

"Mrs. Gifford said whatever you like."

"We'll give you a receipt," Meyer said. He looked at

the bottle of vitamins in Carella's hand. The capsules were jammed into the bottle, each one opaque, and colored purple and black. Meyer stared at them sourly. "You're looking for a third capsule," he said to Carella. "There're a *hundred* of them in that bottle."

He blew his nose then, and began making out a receipt for the vitamins.

8

Dr. Carl Nelson's office was on Hall Avenue in a white apartment building with a green awning that stretched to the curb. Carella and Meyer got there at one o'clock, took the elevator up to the fifth floor, and then announced themselves to a brunette nurse, who said the doctor had a patient with him at the moment, but she'd tell him they were here, wouldn't they please have a seat?

They had a seat.

In ten minutes' time, an elderly lady with a bandage over one eye came out of the doctor's private office. She smiled at the two detectives, either soliciting sympathy for her wound, or offering sympathy for whatever had brought them to see a doctor. Carl Nelson came out of his office with his hand extended.

"How are you?" he said. "Come in, come in. Any news?"

"Well, not really, doctor," Carella said. "We simply wanted to ask you a few questions."

"Happy to help you in any way I can," Nelson said. He turned to his nurse and asked, "When's my next appointment, Rhoda?"

"Two o'clock, doctor."

"No calls except emergencies until then, please," Nelson said, and he led the detectives inside. He sat immediately at his desk, offered Carella and Meyer chairs, and then folded his hands before him in a professionally relaxed, patiently expectant way.

"Are you a general practitioner, Dr. Nelson?" Meyer asked.

"Yes, I am." Nelson smiled. "That's a nasty cold you've got there, Detective Meyer. I hope you're taking something for it."

"I'm taking *everything* for it," Meyer said.

"There're a lot of viruses going around," Nelson said.

"Yes," Meyer agreed.

"Dr. Nelson," Carella said, "I wonder if you'd mind telling us a little about yourself."

"Not at all," Nelson said. "What would you like to know?"

"Well, whatever you feel is pertinent."

"About what? My life? My work? My aspirations?"

"Any of it, or all of it," Carella said pleasantly.

Nelson smiled. "Well . . ." He paused, thinking. "I'm forty-three years old, a native of this city, attended Haworth University here. I was graduated with a B.S. in January of 1944, and got drafted just in time for the assault on Cassino."

"How old were you at the time, Dr. Nelson?"

"Twenty-two."

"Was this Army?"

"Yes. The Medical Corps."

"Were you an officer or an enlisted man?"

"I was a corporal. I was attached to a field hospital in Castelforte. Are you familiar with the country?"

"Vaguely," Carella said.

"There was some fierce fighting," Nelson said briefly. He sighed, dismissing the entire subject. "I was discharged in May of 1946. I began medical school that fall."

"What school was that, Dr. Nelson?"

"Georgetown University. In Washington, D.C."

"And then you came back here to begin practice, is that it?"

"Yes. I opened my own office in 1952."

"This same office?"

"No, my first office was uptown. In Riverhead."

"How long have you been at this location, doctor?"

"Since 1961."

"Are you married?"

"No."

"Have you ever been married?"

"Yes. I was divorced seven years ago."

"Is your former wife alive?"

"Yes."

"Living in this city?"

"No. She lives in San Diego with her new husband. He's an architect there."

"Do you have any children?"

"No."

"You said something about your aspirations, doctor. I wonder . . ."

"Oh." Nelson smiled. "I hope to start a small rest home one day. For elderly people."

"Where?"

"Most likely in Riverhead, where I began practice."

"Now, Dr. Nelson," Carella said, "it's our understanding that you were at home last Wednesday night when Mr. Krantz called to tell you what had happened. Is that correct?"

"Yes, that's correct."

"Were you home all night, Dr. Nelson?"

"Yes, I went home directly from here."

"And what time did you leave here?"

"My usual evening hours are from five o'clock to eight o'clock. I left here last Wednesday night at about ten minutes past eight."

"Can anyone verify that?"

"Yes, Rhoda left with me. Miss Barnaby, my nurse; you just met her. We both left at the same time. You can ask her if you like."

"Where did you go when you left the office?"

"Home. I already said I went directly home."

"Where do you live, Dr. Nelson?"

"On South Fourteenth."

"South Fourteenth, mmm, so it should have taken you,

oh, fifteen minutes at the most to get from here to your house, is that right?''

''That's right. I got home at about eight-thirty.''

''Was anyone there?''

''Just my housekeeper. Mrs. Irene Janlewski. She was preparing my dinner when the call came from the studio. Actually, I didn't need the call.''

''Why not?''

''I'd seen Stan collapse.''

''What do you mean, Dr. Nelson?''

''I was watching the show. I turned it on the moment I got home.''

''At about eight-thirty, is that right?''

''Yes, that's about when I got home.''

''What was happening when you turned on the show?'' Meyer asked.

''Happening?''

''Yes, on the screen,'' Meyer said. He had taken out his black notebook and a pencil and seemed to be taking notes as Nelson spoke. Actually, he was studying the page opposite the one on which he was writing. On that page, in his own hand, was the information George Cooper had given him last Wednesday night at the studio. The folk singers had gone off at eight-thirty-seven, and Gifford had come on immediately afterward, staying on camera with his Hollywood guest for two minutes and twelve seconds. When the guest went off to change . . .

''Stan was doing a commercial when I turned the set on,'' Nelson said. ''A coffee commercial.''

''That would have been at about eight-forty,'' Meyer said.

''Yes, I suppose so.''

''Actually, it would have been exactly eight-thirty-nine and twelve seconds,'' Meyer said, just to be ornery.

''What?'' Nelson asked.

''Which means you didn't turn the set on the moment you got into the house. Not if you got home at eight-thirty.''

''Well, I suppose I talked with Mrs. Janlewski for a few minutes, asked if there were any calls, settled a few household problems, you know.''

"Yes," Meyer said. "The important thing, in any case, is that you were watching Gifford when he got sick."

"Yes, I was."

"Which was at exactly eight-forty-four and seventeen seconds," Meyer said, feeling a wild sense of giddy power.

"Yes," Nelson agreed. "I suppose so."

"What did you think when you saw him collapse?"

"I didn't know what to think. I rushed to the closet for my hat and coat, and was starting out when the telephone rang."

"Who was it?"

"David Krantz."

"And he told you that Gifford was sick, is that right?"

"Right."

"Which you already knew."

"Yes, I already knew it."

"But when you saw Gifford collapse, you didn't know *what* was wrong with him."

"No, I didn't."

"Later on, Dr. Nelson, when I spoke to you at the studio, you seemed certain he'd been poisoned."

"That's true. But that—"

"It was you, in fact, who suggested that we have an autopsy performed."

"That's correct. When I got to the studio, the symptoms were unmistakable. A first-year med student could have diagnosed acute poisoning."

"You didn't know what *kind* of poison, of course."

"How could I?"

"Dr. Nelson," Carella said, "did you ever argue with Stan Gifford?"

"Yes. All friends argue every now and then. It's only acquaintances who never have any differences of opinion."

"What did you argue about?"

"I'm sure I don't remember. Everything. Stan was an alert and well-informed person, with a great many opinions on most things that would concern a thinking man."

"I see. And so you argued about them."

"We *discussed* them, might be a better way of putting it."

"You discussed a wide variety of things, is that right?"

"Yes."

"But you did not *argue* about these things?"

"Yes, we argued, too."

"About matters of general concern."

"Yes."

"Never about anything specific. Never about anything you might consider personal."

"We argued about personal matters, yes."

"Like what?"

"Well, I can't remember any offhand. But I know we argued about personal matters from time to time."

"Try to remember, Dr. Nelson," Carella said.

"Has Melanie told you?" Nelson asked suddenly. "Is that what this is about?"

"Told us what, Dr. Nelson?"

"Are you looking for confirmation, is that it? I can assure you the entire incident was idiotic. Stan was drunk, otherwise he wouldn't have lost his temper that way."

"Tell us about it," Meyer said calmly.

"There'd been a party at his house, and I was dancing with Melanie. Stan had been drinking heavily, and he . . . well, he behaved somewhat ridiculously."

"How did he behave?"

"He accused me of trying to steal his wife, and he . . . he tried to strike me."

"What did *you* do, Dr. Nelson?"

"I defended myself, naturally."

"How? Did you hit him back?"

"No. I simply held up my hands—to ward off his blows, you understand. He was very drunk, really incapable of inflicting any harm."

"When *was* this party, Dr. Nelson?"

"Just after Labor Day. In fact, a week before the show went on the air again. After the summer break, you know. It was a sort of celebration."

"And Stan Gifford thought you were trying to steal his wife, is that right?"

"Yes."

"Merely because you were dancing with her."

"Yes."

"Had you been dancing with her a lot?"

"No. I think that was the second time all evening."

"Then his attack was really unfounded, wasn't it?"

"He was drunk."

"And that's why you feel he attacked you, because he was drunk?"

"And because David Krantz provoked him."

"David Krantz? Was he at the party, too?"

"Yes, most of the people involved with the show were there."

"I see. How did Mr. Krantz provoke him?"

"Oh, you know the stupid jokes some people make."

"No, what sort of jokes, Dr. Nelson?"

"About our dancing together, you know. David Krantz is a barbarian. It's my considered opinion that he's over-sexed and attributes evil thoughts to everyone else in the world, as compensation."

"I see. Then you feel it was Krantz who gave Gifford the idea that you were trying to steal his wife?"

"Yes."

"Why would he do that?"

"He hated Stan. He hates all actors, for that matter. He calls them *cattle*, that's supposed to *endear* them to him, you know."

"How did Gifford feel about *him?*"

"I think the feelings were mutual."

"Gifford hated Krantz, too, is that what you mean?"

"Yes."

"Then why did he take Krantz seriously that night?"

"What do you mean?"

"At the party. When Krantz said you were trying to steal Mrs. Gifford."

"Oh. I don't know. He was drunk. I guess a man will listen to anyone when he's drunk."

"Um-huh," Carella said. He was silent for a moment. Then he asked, "But in spite of this incident, you remained his personal physician, is that right?"

"Oh, of *course*. Stan apologized to me the very next day."

"And you continued to be friends?"

"Yes, certainly. I don't even know why Melanie brought this up. I don't see what bearing—"

"She didn't," Meyer said.

"Oh. Well, who told you about it then? Was it Krantz? I wouldn't put it past him. He's a goddamn troublemaker."

"No one told us, actually," Meyer said. "This is the first we've heard of the incident."

"Oh." Nelson paused. "Well, it doesn't matter. I'd rather you heard it from me than from someone else who was at the party."

"That's very sensible of you, Dr. Nelson. You're being most cooperative." Carella paused. "If it's all right with you, we'll simply verify with your nurse that you left here with her at about ten minutes past eight last Wednesday night. And we'll— "

"Yes, you certainly may verify it with her."

"And we'd also like to call your housekeeper—with your permission, of course—to verify that you arrived home at about eight-thirty, as you say, and remained there until after Krantz's phone call."

"Certainly. My nurse will give you my home number."

"Thank you, Dr. Nelson. You've been very cooperative," Carella said, and they went out to talk to Miss Barnaby, who told them the doctor had arrived at the office at four-forty-five last Wednesday afternoon and had not left until office hours were over, at ten minutes past eight. She was absolutely certain about this because she and the doctor had left at the same time. She gave them the doctor's home number so that they could speak to Mrs. Janlewski, the housekeeper, and they thanked her politely and went downstairs and then out of the building.

"He's very cooperative," Carella said.

"Yes, he's very very cooperative," Meyer agreed.

"Let's put a tail on him," Carella said.

"I've got a better idea," Meyer said. "Let's put a tail on him and Krantz *both*."

"Good idea."

"You agree?"

"Sure."

"You think one of them did it?"

"I think you did it," Carella said, and suddenly slipped his handcuffs from his belt and snapped one of them onto Meyer's wrist. "Come along now, no tricks," he said.

"You know what a guy needs like a hole in the head when he's got a bad cold?" Meyer said.

"What?"

"A partner who plays jokes."

"I'm not playing jokes, mister," Carella said, his eyes narrowing. "I happen to know that Stan Gifford took out a seven-million-dollar insurance policy on his life, payable to your wife Sarah as beneficiary in the event that he died on any Wednesday between eight-thirty and nine-thirty P.M. during the month of October. I further happen to know—"

"Oh, boy," Meyer said, "start up with *goyim*."

Back at the squadroom, they made two telephone calls.

The first was to Municipal Life, where they learned that Stanley Gifford's insurance policy had been written only a year and a half ago, and contained a clause that read, "Death within two years from the date of issue of this policy, from suicide while sane or insane, shall limit the company's liability hereunder to the amount of the premiums actually paid hereon."

The second was to Mr. Salvatore Di Palma, Gifford's lawyer, who promptly confirmed that Melanie Gifford had not been familiar with the terms of her husband's will.

"Why do you want to know?" he asked.

"We're investigating his murder," Carella said.

"There's nothing in Stan's will that would have caused Melanie to even *consider* murder," Di Palma said.

"Why do you say that?"

"Because I know what's in the will."

"Can you tell us?"

"I would not regard it as appropriate for me to reveal the contents of the will to any person until it has first been read to Mr. Gifford's widow."

"We're investigating a murder," Carella said.

"Look, take my word for it," Di Palma said. "There's nothing here to indicate—"

"You mean he doesn't leave her anything?"

"Did I say that?"

"No, *I* said it," Carella said. "Does he, or doesn't he?"

"You're twisting my arm," Di Palma said, and then chuckled. He liked talking to Italians. They were the only civilized people in the world.

"Come on," Carella said, "help a working man."

"Okay, but you didn't hear it from me," Di Palma said, still chuckling. "Stan came in early last month, asked me to revise his will."

"Why?"

"He didn't say. The will now leaves his house and his personal property to Mrs. Adelaide Garfein, that's his mother, she's a widow in Poughkeepsie, New York."

"Go ahead."

"It leaves one-third of the remainder of his estate to the American Guild of Variety Artists, one-third to the Academy of Television Arts and Sciences, and one-third to the Damon Runyon Cancer Fund."

"And Melanie?"

"Zero," Di Palma said. "That's what the change was all about. He cut her out of it completely."

"Thank you very much."

"For what?" Di Palma said, and chuckled again. "I didn't tell you anything, did I?"

"You didn't say a word," Carella said. "Thanks again."

"Don't mention it," Di Palma said, and hung up.

"So?" Meyer asked.

"He left her nothing," Carella said. "Changed the will early last month."

"Nothing?"

"Nothing." Carella paused. "That's pretty funny, don't you think? I mean, here's this sweet woman who had led a full and happy life with her husband, and who wants to take us upstairs to show us all her furs and jewelry and such—and just last month he cuts her out of his will. That's pretty funny, I think."

"Yeah, especially since just last month he also took a

sock at our doctor friend and accused him of trying to steal his wife.''

''Yeah, that's a very funny coincidence,'' Carella said.

''Maybe he really *believed* Nelson was trying to steal his wife.''

''Maybe so.''

''Mmm,'' Meyer said. He thought for a moment and then said, ''But she still looks clean, Steve. She doesn't get a cent either way.''

''Unless we find a murderer, in which case it's no longer suicide, in which case she collects a hundred G's from the insurance company.''

''Yeah, but that *still* leaves her out. Because if she's the one who did it, she wouldn't plan it to look like a *suicide*, would she?''

''What do you mean?''

''This thing looks exactly like a suicide. Listen, for all I know, it *is* one.''

''So?''

''So if you're hoping to get a hundred thousand dollars on an insurance policy that has a suicide clause, you're sure as hell not going to plan a murder that looks like a suicide, right?''

''Right.''

''So?'' Meyer said.

''So Melanie Gifford looks clean.''

''Yeah.''

''Guess what I found out?'' Carella said.

''What?''

''Gifford's real name is Garfein.''

''Yeah?''

''Yeah.''

''So what? *My* real name is Rock Hudson.''

9

Considering the number of *human* killings that took place daily in the five separate sections of the city, Kling was surprised to discover that the city could boast of only one slaughterhouse. Apparently the guiding fathers and the Butchers Union (who gave him the information) were averse to killing animals within the city limits. The single slaughterhouse was on Boswell Avenue in Calm's Point, and it specialized in the slaughtering of lambs. Most of the city's killing, as Grossman had surmised, was done in four separate slaughterhouses across the river, in the next state. Since Calm's Point was closest, Kling hit the one on Boswell Avenue first. He was armed with the list he had compiled at the lab earlier that day, together with the drawing he had received from the BCI. He didn't know exactly what he was looking for, or exactly what he hoped to discover. He had never been inside a slaughterhouse before.

After visiting the one on Calm's Point, he never wanted to step inside another one as long as he lived. Unfortunately, there were four more to check across the river.

He was used to blood; a cop gets used to blood. He was used to the sight of human beings bleeding in a hundred different ways from a thousand different wounds, he was used to all that. He had been witness to sudden attacks with razor blades or knives, pistols or shotguns, had seen the body case torn or punctured, the blood beginning to flow or spurt. He had seen them dead and bleeding, and he had seen them alive and in the midst of attack—bleeding. But he had never seen an animal killed before, and the sight made him want to retch. He could barely concentrate on what the head butcher was telling him. The bleating of the lambs rang in his ears, the stench of blood filled the air. The head butcher looked at the drawing Kling extended, leaving a bloody thumbprint on the celluloid sleeve, and shook his head. Behind him the animals shrieked.

The air outside was cold, it drilled the nostrils. He sucked breath after breath into his lungs, deeply savoring each cleansing rush. He did not want to go across that river, but he went. Forsaking lunch, because he knew he would not be able to keep it down, he hit two more slaughterhouses in succession and—finding nothing—grimly prepared to visit the next two on his list.

There is an intuitive feel to detection, and the closest thing to sudden truth—outside of fiction—is the dawning awareness of a cop when he is about to make a fresh discovery. The moment Kling drove onto the dock he knew he would hit pay dirt. The knowledge was sudden and fierce. He stepped out of the police sedan with a faint vague smile on his face, looking up at the huge white sign across the top of the building, facing the river, PURLEY BROTHERS, INC. He stood in the center of the open dock, an area the size of a baseball diamond, and took his time surveying the location, while all the while the rising knowledge clamored within him, this is it, this is it, this is it.

One side of the dock was open to the waterfront. Beyond the two marine gasoline pumps at the water's edge, Kling could see across the river to where the towers of the city were silhouetted against the grey October sky. His eye lingered on the near distance for a moment, and then he swung his head to the right, where a half-dozen fishing boats were tied up, fishermen dumping their nets and their baskets, leaping onto the dock and then sitting with their booted legs hanging over its edge while they scraped and cleaned their fish and transferred them to fresh baskets lined with newspapers. The grin on his face widened because he knew for certain now that this was pay dirt, that everything would fall into place here on this dock.

He turned his attention back to the slaughterhouse that formed almost one complete side of the rectangular dock area. Gulls shrieked in the air over the river where waste material poured from an open pipe. Railroad tracks fed the rear of the brick building, a siding that ran from the yards some five hundred feet back from the dock. He walked to the tracks and began following them to the building.

They led directly to the animal pens, empty now, along-side of which were the metal entrance doors to the slaughterhouse. He knew what he would find on the floor inside; he had seen the floors of three such places already.

The manager was a man named Joe Brady, and he was more than delighted to help Kling. He took him into a small, glass-partitioned office overlooking the killing floor (Kling sat with his back to the glass) and then accepted the drawing Kling handed to him, and pondered it for several moments, and then asked, "What is he, a nigger?"

"No," Kling said. "He's a white man."

"You said he attacked a girl, didn't you?"

"Yes, that's right."

"And he ain't a nigger?" Brady shook his head.

"You can see from the drawing that he's white," Kling said. An annoyed tone had crept into his voice. Brady did not seem to notice.

"Well, it's hard to tell from a drawing," he said. "I mean, the way the shading is done here, look, right here, you see what I mean? That could be a nigger."

"Mr. Brady," Kling said flatly, "I do not like that word."

"What word?" Brady asked.

"Nigger."

"Oh, come on," Brady said, "don't get on your high horse. We got a half a dozen niggers working here, they're all nice guys, what the hell's the matter with you?"

"The word offends me," Kling said. "Cut it out."

Brady abruptly handed back the drawing. "I've never seen this guy in my life," he said. "If you're finished here, I got to get back to work."

"He doesn't work here?"

"No."

"Are all of your employees full-time men?"

"All of them."

"No part-time workers, maybe somebody who worked here for just a few days—"

"I know everybody who works here," Brady said. "That guy don't work here."

"Is he someone who might possibly make deliveries here?"

"What kind of deliveries?"

"I don't know. Maybe—"

"The only thing we get delivered here is animals."

"I'm sure you get other things delivered here, Mr. Brady."

"Nothing," Brady said, and he rose from behind his desk. "I got to get back to work."

"Sit down, Mr. Brady," Kling said. His voice was harsh.

Surprised, Brady looked at him with rising eyebrows, ready to *really* take offense.

"I said sit down. Now go ahead."

"Listen, mister—" Brady started.

"No, you listen, mister," Kling said. "I'm investigating an assault, and I have good reason to believe this man"—he tapped the drawing—"was somewhere around here last Friday. Now, I don't like your goddamn attitude, Mr. Brady, and if you'd like the inconvenience of answering some questions uptown at the station house instead of here in your nice cozy office overlooking all that killing out there, that's just fine with me. So why don't you get your hat and we'll just take a little ride, okay?"

"What for?" Brady said.

Kling did not answer. He sat grimly on the side of the desk opposite Brady and studied him coldly. Brady looked deep into his eyes.

"The only thing we get delivered here is animals," he said again.

"Then how'd the paper cups get here?"

"Huh?"

"On the water cooler," Kling said. "Don't brush me off, Mr. Brady, I'm goddamn good and sore."

"Okay, okay," Brady said.

"Okay! Who delivers stuff here?"

"A lot of people. But I know most of them, and I don't recognize that picture."

"Are there any deliveries made that you would not ordinarily see?"

"What do you mean?"

"Does anything come into this building that you personally would not check?"

"I check anything that goes in or out. What do you mean? You mean *personal* things, too?"

"Personal things?"

"Things that have nothing to do with the business?"

"What'd you have in mind, Mr. Brady?"

"Well, some of the guys order lunch from the diner across the dock. They got guys working there who bring the lunch over. Or coffee sometimes. I got my own little hot plate here in the office, so I don't have to send out for coffee, and also I bring my lunch from home. So I don't usually get to see the guys who make the deliveries."

"Thank you," Kling said, and rose.

Brady could not resist a parting shot. "Anyway," he said, "most of them delivery guys are niggers."

The air outside was clean, blowing fresh and wet off the river. Kling sighted the diner on the opposite end of the dock rectangle and quickly began walking toward it. It was set in a row of shops that slowly came into sharper focus as he moved closer to them. The two shops flanking the diner were occupied by a plumber and a glazier.

He took out his notebook and consulted it: suet, sawdust, blood, animal hair, fish scale, putty, wood splinter, metal filings, peanut, and gasoline. The only item he could not account for was the peanut, but maybe he'd find one in the diner. He was hopeful, in fact, of finding something more than just a peanut inside. He was hopeful of finding the man who had stopped at the slaughterhouse and stepped into the suet, blood and sawdust to which the animal hair had later clung when he crossed the pens outside. He was hopeful of finding the man who had walked along the creo-soted railroad tracks, picking up a wood splinter in the sticky mess on his heel. He was hopeful of finding the man who had stopped on the edge of the dock where the fisher-men were cleaning fish, and later walked through a small puddle of gasoline near the marine pumps, and then into the glazier's where he had acquired the dot of putty, and the plumber's where the copper filings had been added to the rest of the glopis. He was hopeful of finding the man who had beaten Cindy senseless, and the possibil-ity seemed strong that this man made deliveries for the diner. Who else could wander so easily in and out of so many places? Kling unbuttoned his coat and reassuringly touched the butt of his revolver. Briskly, he walked to the door of the diner and entered.

The smell of greasy food assailed his nostrils. He had not eaten since breakfast, and the aroma combined with his slaughterhouse memories to bring on a feeling of nausea. He took a seat at the counter and ordered a cup of coffee, wanting to look over the personnel before he showed his drawing to anyone. There were two men behind the counter, one white and one colored. Neither looked anything at all like the drawing. Behind a pass-through into the kitchen, he caught a glimpse of another white man as he put down a hamburger for pickup. He was not the suspect, either. Two Negro delivery boys in white jackets were sitting in a booth near the cash register, where a baldheaded white man sat picking his teeth with a matchstick. Kling assumed he had seen every employee in the place, with the possible exception of the short-order cook. He finished his coffee, went to the cash register, showed his shield to the baldheaded man and said, "I'd like to talk to the manager, please."

"I'm the manager and the owner both," the baldheaded man said. "Myron Krepps, how do you do?"

"I'm Detective Kling. I wonder if you would take a look at this picture and tell me if you know the man."

"I'd be more than happy to," Krepps said. "Did he do something?"

"Yes," Kling said.

"May I ask what it is he done?"

"Well, that's not important," Kling said. He took the drawing from its envelope and handed it to Krepps. Krepps cocked his head to one side and studied it.

"Does he work here?" Kling asked.

"Nope," Krepps said.

"Has he ever worked here?"

"Nope," Krepps said.

"Have you ever seen him in the diner?"

Krepps paused. "Is this something serious?"

"Yes," Kling said, and then immediately asked, "Why?" He could not have said what instinct provoked him into pressing the issue, unless it was the slight hesitation in Krepps's voice as he asked his question.

"How serious?" Krepps said.

"He beat up a young girl," Kling said.

"Oh."

"Is that serious enough?"

"That's pretty serious," Krepps admitted.

"Serious enough for you to tell me who he is?"

"I thought it was a minor thing," Krepps said. "For minor things, who needs to be a good citizen?"

"Do you know this man, Mr. Krepps?"

"Yes, I seen him around."

"Have you seen him here in the diner?"

"Yes."

"How often?"

"When he makes his rounds."

"What do you mean?"

"He goes to all the places on the dock here."

"Doing what?"

"I wouldn't get him in trouble for what he does," Krepps said. "As far as I'm concerned, it's no crime what he does. The city is unrealistic, that's all."

"What is it that he does, Mr. Krepps?"

"It's only that you say he beat up a young girl. That's serious. For that, I don't have to protect him."

"Why does he come here, Mr. Krepps? Why does he go to all the places on the dock?"

"He collects for the numbers," Krepps said. "Whoever

wants to play the numbers, they give him their bets when he comes around.''

''What's his name?''

''They call him Cookie.''

''Cookie what?''

''I don't know his last name. Just Cookie. He comes to collect for the numbers.''

''Do you sell peanuts, Mr. Krepps?''

''What? Peanuts?''

''Yes.''

''No, I don't sell peanuts. I carry some chocolates and some Life Savers and some chewing gum, but no peanuts. Why? You like peanuts?''

''Is there any place on the dock where I can get some?''

''Not on the dock,'' Krepps said.

''Where then?''

''Up the street. There's a bar. You can get peanuts there.''

''Thank you,'' Kling said. ''You've been very helpful.''

''Good, I'm glad,'' Krepps said. ''Now, please, would you mind paying for the coffee you drank?''

The front plate-glass window of the bar was painted a dull green. Bold white letters spelled out the name, BUDDY'S, arranged in a somewhat sloppy semicircle in the center of the glass. Kling walked into the bar and directly to the phone booth some five feet beyond the single entrance door. He took a dime from his pocket, put it in the slot, and dialed his own home phone. While the phone rang unanswered on the other end, he simulated a lively conversation and simultaneously cased the bar. He did not recognize Cindy's attacker among any of the men sitting at the bar itself or in the booths. He hung up, fished his dime from the return chute, and walked up to the bar. The bartender looked at him curiously. He was either a college kid who had wandered into the waterfront area by accident—or else he was a cop. Kling settled the speculation at once by producing his shield.

''Detective Bert Kling,'' he said. ''87th Squad.''

The bartender studied the shield with an unwavering

eye—he was used to bulls wandering in and out of his fine
establishment—and then asked in a very polite, prep-school
voice, "What is it that you wish, Detective Kling?"

Kling did not answer at once. Instead, he scooped a
handful of peanuts from the bowl on the bar top, put
several into his mouth, and began chewing noisily. The
proper thing to do, he supposed, was to inquire about
some violation or other, garbage cans left outside, serving
alcohol to minors, any damn thing to throw the bartender
off base. The next thing to do was have the lieutenant
assign another man or men to a stakeout of the bar, and
simply pick up Cookie the next time he wandered in. That
was the proper procedure, and Kling debated using it as he
munched on his peanuts and stared silently at the bartender. The only trouble with picking up Cookie, of course,
was that Cindy Forrest had been frightened half to death of
him. How could you persuade a girl who'd been beaten
senseless that it was in her own interest to identify the man
who had attacked her? Kling kept munching his peanuts.
The bartender kept watching him.

"Would you like a beer or something, Detective Kling?"
he asked.

"You the owner?"

"I'm Buddy. You want a beer?"

"Uh-uh," Kling said, chewing. "On duty."

"Well, was there something on your mind?" Buddy
asked.

Kling nodded. He had made his decision. He began
baiting his trap. "Cookie been in today?"

"Cookie who?"

"You get a lot of people named Cookie in here?"

"I don't know *anybody* named Cookie in here," Buddy
said.

"Yeah, you do," Kling said, and nodded. He scooped
up another handful of peanuts. "Don't you know him?"

"No."

"That's a shame." Kling began munching peanuts again.
Buddy continued watching him. "You're sure you don't
know him?"

"Never heard of him."

"That's too bad," Kling said. "We want him. We want him real bad."

"What for?"

"He beat up a girl."

"Yeah?"

"Yeah. Sent her to the hospital."

"No kidding?"

"That's right," Kling said. "We've been searching the whole damn city for him." He paused, and then took a wild gamble. "Couldn't find him at the address we had in the Lousy File, but we happen to know he comes in here a lot."

"How do you happen to know that?"

Kling smiled. "We've got ways."

"Mmm," Buddy said noncommittally.

"We'll get him," Kling said, and again he took a wild gamble. "The girl identified his picture. Soon as we pick him up, goodbye, Charlie."

"He's got a record, huh?"

"No," Kling answered. "No record."

Buddy leaned forward slightly, ready to pounce. "No record, huh?"

"Nope."

"Then how'd you get his picture for the girl to identify?" Buddy said, and suddenly smiled.

"He's in the numbers racket," Kling said. Idly, he popped another peanut into his mouth.

"So?"

"We've got a file on them."

"On who?"

"On half the guys involved with numbers in this city."

"Yeah?" Buddy said. His eyes had narrowed to a squint. It was plain to see that he did not trust Kling and was searching for a flaw in what he was being told.

"Sure," Kling said. "Addresses, pictures, even prints on some of them."

"Yeah?" Buddy said again.

"Yeah."

"What for?"

"Waiting for them to step out of line."

"What do you mean?"

"I mean something bigger than numbers. Something we can lock them up for and throw away the key."

"Oh." Buddy nodded. He was convinced. This, he understood. The devious ways of cops, he understood. Kling tried to keep his face blank. He picked up another handful of peanuts.

"Cookie's finally stepped over the line. Once we get him, the girl takes another look, and bingo! First-degree assault."

"He used a weapon?"

"Nope, his hands. But he tried to kill her nonetheless." Buddy shrugged.

"We'll get him, all right," Kling said. "We know who he is, so it's just a matter of time."

"Yeah, well." Buddy shrugged.

"All we have to do is find him, that's all. The rest is easy."

"Yeah, well, sometimes finding a person can be extremely difficult," Buddy said, reactivating his prep-school voice.

"I'm going to give you a word of warning, friend," Kling said.

"What's that?"

"Keep your mouth shut about my being in here."

"Who would I tell?"

"I don't know *who* you'd tell, but it better be *nobody.*"

"Why would I want to obstruct justice?" Buddy said, an offended look coming onto his face. "If this Cookie person beat up a girl, why then good luck to you in finding him."

"I appreciate your sentiments."

"Sure." Buddy paused, and glanced down at the peanut bowl. "You going to eat *all* of those, or what?"

"Remember what I told you," Kling said, hoping he wasn't overdoing it. "Keep your mouth shut. If this leaks, and we trace it back to you . . ."

"Nothing leaks around here but the beer tap," Buddy answered, and moved away when someone at the other end of the bar signaled him. Kling sat a moment longer, and then rose, put another handful of peanuts into his mouth, and walked out.

On the pavement outside, he permitted himself a smile.

The item appeared in both afternoon newspapers later that day.

It was small and hardly noticeable, buried as it was in a morass of print on the fourth page of both papers. Its headline was brief but eye-catching:

Witnesses to Beating Balk

Two witnesses to the brutal beating of Patrolman Ronald Fairchild last Wednesday, October 11, refused today to identify a photograph of the alleged attacker.

The picture was taken from a police file of "numbers racketeers" and had been shown previously to another victim of the same suspect. Miss Cynthia Forrest, recuperating from a bad beating at Elizabeth Rushmore Hospital here, positively identified the photograph and agreed to testify against the known suspect when he is apprehended.

Patrolman Critical

Detective-Lieutenant Peter

Byrnes, whose 87th Squad is investigating both assaults, commented today, "The apathy of these other witnesses is appalling. Patrolman Fairchild has been in coma and on the critical list at Buena Vista Hospital ever since he was admitted last week. If this man dies, we are dealing with a homicide here. Were it not for decent people like Miss Forrest, this city would never get to prosecute a criminal case."

Byrnes read the article in the privacy of his corner office, and then looked up at Kling, who was standing on the other side of his desk, beaming with the pride of authorship.

"Is Fairchild really on the critical list?" he asked.

"Nope," Kling answered.

"Suppose our man checks?"

"Let him check. I've alerted Buena Vista."

Byrnes nodded and looked at the article again. He put it aside then, and said, "You made me sound like a jerk."

10

Meyer and Carella were in the squadroom when Kling came out of the lieutenant's office.

"How you doing?" Carella asked him.

"So-so. We were just looking over the cheese."

"What cheese?"

"Ah-ha," Kling said mysteriously, and left.

"When did the lab say they'd call back on those vitamin capsules?" Carella asked.

"Sometime today," Meyer answered.

"When today? It's past five already."

"Don't jump on me," Meyer said, and rose from his desk to walk to the water cooler. The telephone rang. Carella lifted it from the cradle.

"87th Squad, Carella," he said.

"Steve, this is Bob O'Brien."

"Yeah, what's up, Bob?"

"How long do you want me to stick with this Nelson guy?"

"Where are you?"

"Outside his house. I tailed him from his office to the hospital and then here."

"What hospital?"

"General Presbyterian."

"What was he doing there?"

"Search me. Most doctors are connected with hospitals, aren't they?"

"I guess so. When did he leave his office?"

"This afternoon, after visiting hours."

"What time was that?"

"A little after two."

"And he went directly to the hospital?"

"Yeah. He drives a little red MG."

"What time did he leave the hospital?"

"About a half hour ago."

"And went straight home?"

"Right. You think he's bedded down for the night?"

"I don't know. Call me in an hour or so, will you?"

"Right. Where'll you be? Home?"

"No, we'll be here awhile yet."

"Okay," O'Brien said, and hung up. Meyer came back to his desk with a paper cup full of water. He propped it against his telephone, and then opened his desk drawer and took out a long cardboard strip of brightly colored capsules.

"What's that?" Carella asked.

"For my cold," Meyer said, and popped one of the capsules out of its cellophane wrapping. He put it into his mouth and washed it down with water. The phone rang again. Meyer picked it up.

"87th Squad, Meyer."

"Meyer, this is Andy Parker. I'm still with Krantz, just checking in. He's in a cocktail lounge with a girl has boobs like watermelons."

"What size, would you say?" Meyer asked.

"Huh? How the hell do I know?"

"Okay, just stick with him. Call in again later, will you?"

"I'm tired," Parker said.

"So am I."

"Yeah, but I'm *really* tired," Parker said, and hung up. Meyer replaced the phone on its cradle. "Parker," he said. "Krantz is out drinking."

"That's nice," Carella said. "You want to send out for some food?"

"With this case, I'm not very hungry," Carella said.

"There should be mathematics."

"What do you mean?"

"To a case. There should be the laws of mathematics. I
don't like cases that defy addition and subtraction."

"What the hell was Bert grinning about when he left?"

"I don't know. He grins a lot," Meyer said, and
shrugged. "I like two and two to make four. I like suicide
to be suicide."

"You think this is suicide?"

"No. That's what I mean. I don't like suicide to be
murder. I like mathematics."

"I failed geometry in high school," Carella said.

"Yeah?"

"Yeah."

"Our facts are right," Meyer said, "and the facts add
up to suicide. But I don't like the feel."

"The feel is wrong," Carella agreed.

"That's right, the feel is wrong. The feel is murder."

The telephone rang. Meyer picked it up. "87th Squad,
Meyer," he said. "You again? What now?" He listened.
"Yeah? Yeah? Well, I don't know, we'll check it. Okay,
stick with it. Right." He hung up.

"Who?" Carella said.

"Bob O'Brien. He says a blue Thunderbird just pulled
up to Nelson's house, and a blond woman got out. He
wanted to know if Melanie Gifford drives a blue Thunderbird."

"I don't know what the hell she drives, do you?"

"No."

"Motor Vehicle Bureau's closed, isn't it?"

"We can get them on the night line."

"I think we'd better."

Meyer shrugged. "Nelson is a friend of the family. It's
perfectly reasonable for her to be visiting him."

"Yeah, I know," Carella said. "What's the number
there?"

"Here you go," Meyer said, and flipped open his telephone pad. "Of course, there was that business at Gifford's
party."

"The argument, you mean?" Carella said, dialing.

"Yeah, when Gifford took a sock at the doctor."

"Yeah." Carella nodded. "It's ringing."

"But Gifford was drunk."

"Yeah. Hello," Carella said into the phone. "Steve Carella, Detective/Second, 87th Squad. Checking automobile registration for Mrs. Melanie Gifford, Larksview. Right, I'll wait. What? No, that's Gifford, with a G. Right." He covered the mouthpiece. "Doesn't Bob know what she looks like?" he asked.

"How would he?"

"That's right. This goddamn case is making me dizzy." He glanced down at the cardboard strip of capsules on Meyer's desk. "What's that stuff you're taking, anyway?"

"It's supposed to be good," Meyer said. "Better than all that other crap I've been using."

Carella looked up at the wall clock.

"Anyway, I only have to take them twice a day," Meyer said.

"Hello," Carella said into the phone. "Yep, go ahead. Blue Thunderbird convertible, 1964. Right, thank you." He hung up. "You heard?"

"I heard."

"That's pretty interesting, huh?"

"That's *very* interesting."

"What do you suppose old Melanie Wistful wants with our doctor friend?"

"Maybe she's got a cold, too," Meyer said.

"Maybe so." Carella sighed. "Why only twice?"

"Huh?"

"Why do you only have to take them twice a day?"

Five minutes later, Carella was placing a call to Detective-Lieutenant Sam Grossman at his home in Majesta.

Bob O'Brien was standing across the street from Nelson's brownstone on South Fourteenth when Meyer and Carella arrived. The red MG was parked in front of the doorway, and behind that was Melanie Gifford's blue Thunderbird. Meyer and Carella walked up to where he stood with his shoulders hunched and his hands in his pockets. He recognized them immediately, but only nodded in greeting.

"Getting pretty chilly," he said.

"Mmm. She still in there?"

"Yep. The way I figure it, he's got the whole building. Ground floor is the entry, first floor must be the kitchen, dining and living room area, and the top floor's the bedrooms."

"How the hell'd you figure that?" Meyer asked.

"Ground-floor light went on when the woman arrived—is she Mrs. Gifford?"

"She is."

"Mmm-huh," O'Brien said, "and out again immediately afterwards. The lights on the first floor were on until just a little while ago. An older woman came out at about seven. I figure she's either the cook or the housekeeper or both."

"So they're alone in there, huh?"

"Yeah. Light went on upstairs just about ten minutes after the old lady left. See that small window? I figure that's the john, don't you?"

"Yeah, must be."

"That went on first, and then off, and then the light in the big window went on. That's a bedroom, sure as hell."

"What do you suppose they're doing in there?" Meyer asked.

"I know what *I'd* be doing in there," O'Brien said.

"Why don't you go home?" Carella said.

"You don't need me?"

"No. Go on, we'll see you tomorrow."

"You going in?"

"Yeah."

"You sure you won't need me to take pictures?"

"Ha ha," Meyer said, and then followed Carella, who had already begun crossing the street. They paused on the front step. Carella found the doorbell and rang it. There was no answer. He rang it again. Meyer stepped back off the stoop. The lights on the first floor went on.

"He's coming down," Meyer whispered.

"Let him come down," Carella said. "Second murderer."

"Huh?"

"Macbeth, Act III, scene 3."

"Boy," Meyer said, and the entry lights went on. The front door opened a moment later.

"Dr. Nelson?" Carella said.

"Yes?" The doctor seemed surprised, but not particularly annoyed. He was wearing a black silk robe, and his feet were encased in slippers.

"I wonder if we might come in," Carella said.

"Well, I was just getting ready for bed."

"This won't take a moment."

"Well . . ."

"You're alone, aren't you, doctor?"

"Yes, of course," Nelson said.

"May we come in?"

"Well . . . well, yes. I suppose so. But I *am* tired, and I hope—"

"We'll be brief as we possibly can," Carella said, and he walked into the house. There was a couch in the entry, a small table before it. A mirror was on the wall opposite the door; a shelf for mail was fastened to the wall below it. Nelson did not invite them upstairs. He put his hands in the pockets of his robe, and made it clear from his stance that he did not intend moving farther into the house than the entry hall.

"I've got a cold," Meyer said.

Nelson's eyebrows went up just a trifle.

"I've been trying everything," Meyer continued. "I just started on some new stuff. I hope it works."

Nelson frowned. "Excuse me, Detective Meyer," he said, "but did you come here to discuss your—"

Carella reached into his jacket pocket. When he extended his hand to Nelson, there was a purple-and-black gelatin capsule on the palm.

"Do you know what this is, Dr. Nelson?" he asked.

"It looks like a vitamin capsule," Nelson answered.

"It is, to be specific, a PlexCin capsule, the combination of Vitamin C and B-complex that Stan Gifford was using."

"Oh, yes," Nelson said, nodding.

"In fact, to be more specific, it is a capsule taken from the bottle of vitamins Gifford kept in his home."

"Yes?" Nelson said. He seemed extremely puzzled. He seemed to be wondering exactly where Carella was leading.

"We sent the bottle of capsules to Lieutenant Grossman at the lab this afternoon," Carella said. "No poison in any of them. Only vitamins."

"But I've got a cold," Meyer said.

Nelson frowned.

"And Detective Meyer's cold led us to call Lieutenant Grossman again, just for the fun of it. He agreed to meet us at the lab, Dr. Nelson. We've been down there for the past few hours. Sam—that's Lieutenant Grossman—had some interesting things to tell us, and we wanted your ideas. We want to be as specific about this as possible, you see, since there are a great many specifics in the Gifford case. Isn't that right?"

"Yes, I suppose so."

"The specific poison, for example, and the specific dose, and the specific speed of the poison, and the specific dissolving rate of a gelatin capsule, isn't that right?"

"Yes, that's right," Nelson said.

"You're an attending physician at General Presbyterian, aren't you, Dr. Nelson?"

"Yes, I am."

"We spoke to the pharmacist there just a little while ago. He tells us they stock strophanthin in its crystalline powder form, oh, maybe three or four grains of it. The rest is in ampules, and even that isn't kept in any great amount."

"That's very interesting. But what—"

"Open the capsule, Dr. Nelson."

"What?"

"The vitamin capsule. Open it. It comes apart. Go ahead. The size is a double-O, Dr. Nelson. You know that, don't you?"

"I would assume it was either an O or a double-O."

"But let's be specific. This specific capsule that contains the vitamins Gifford habitually took is a double-O."

"All right then, it's a double-O."

"Open it."

Nelson sat on the couch, put the capsule on the low

table, and carefully pulled one part from the other. A sifting of powder fell onto the table top.

"That's the vitamin compound, Dr. Nelson. The same stuff that's in every one of those capsules in Gifford's bottle. Harmless. In fact, to be specific, beneficial. Isn't that right?"

"That's right."

"Take another look at the capsule." Nelson looked. "No, Dr. Nelson, *inside* the capsule. Do you see anything?"

"Why . . . there . . . there appears to be another capsule inside it."

"Why, yes!" Carella said. "Upon my soul, there *does* appear to be another capsule inside it. As a matter of fact, Dr. Nelson, it is a number *three* gelatin capsule, which, as you see, fits very easily into the large double-O capsule. We made this sample at the lab." He lifted the larger capsule from the table and then shook out the rest of its vitamin contents. The smaller capsule fell onto the table top. Using his forefinger, Carella pushed the smaller capsule away from the small mound of vitamins and said, "The third capsule, Dr. Nelson."

"I don't know what you mean."

"We were looking for a third capsule, you see. Since the one Gifford took at lunch couldn't possibly have killed him. Now, Dr. Nelson, if this smaller capsule were loaded with two grains of strophanthin and placed inside the larger capsule, *that* could have killed him, don't you think?"

"Certainly, but it would have—"

"Yes, Dr. Nelson?"

"Well, it seems to me that . . . that the smaller capsule would have dissolved very rapidly, too. I mean—"

"You mean, don't you, Dr. Nelson, that if the outside capsule took six minutes to dissolve, the inside capsule might take, oh, let's say another three or four or five or however many minutes to dissolve. Is that what you mean?"

"Yes."

"So that doesn't really change anything, does it? The poison still would have had to be taken just before Gifford went on."

"Yes, I would imagine so."

"But I have a cold," Meyer said.

"Yes, and he's taking some capsules of his own," Carrella said, smiling. "Only has to take two a day because the drug is released slowly over a period of twelve hours. They're called time-release capsules, Dr. Nelson. I'm sure you're familiar with them." Nelson seemed as if he were about to rise, and Carella instantly said, "Stay where you are, Dr. Nelson, we're not finished."

Meyer smiled and said, "Of course, my capsules were produced commercially. I imagine it would be impossible to duplicate a time-release capsule without manufacturing facilities, wouldn't it, Dr. Nelson?"

"I would imagine so."

"Well, to be specific," Carella said, "Lieutenant Sam Grossman said it *was* impossible to duplicate such a capsule. But he remembered experiments from way back in his Army days, Dr. Nelson, when some of the doctors in his outfit were playing around with what is called enteric coating. Did the doctors in your outfit try it, too? Are you familiar with the expression 'enteric coating,' Dr. Nelson?"

"Of course I am," Nelson said, and he rose, and Carella leaned across the table and put his hands on the doctor's shoulders and slammed him down onto the couch again.

"Enteric coating," Carella said, "as it specifically applies to this small *inside* capsule, Dr. Nelson, means that if the capsule had been immersed for exactly thirty seconds in a one-percent solution of formaldehyde, and then allowed to dry—"

"What is all this? Why are you—"

"—and then held for two weeks to allow the formaldehyde to act upon the gelatin, hardening it, then the—"

"I don't know what you mean!"

"I mean that a capsule treated in just that way would *not* dissolve in normal gastric juices for at least *three* hours, Dr. Nelson, by which time it would have left the stomach. And after that, it would dissolve in the small intestine within a period of *five* hours. So you see, Dr. Nelson, we're not working with six minutes any more. Only the outside capsule would have dissolved that quickly. We're working with anywhere from three to eight *hours*. We're working with a soft outer shell and a hard inner nucleus containing two full grains of poison. To be specific, Dr. Nelson, we are working with the capsule Gifford undoubtedly took at lunch on the day he was murdered."

Nelson shook his head. "I don't know what you're talking about," he said. "I had nothing to with any of this."

"Ahhh, Dr. Nelson," Carella said. "Did we forget to mention that the pharmacy at General Presbyterian has a record of all drugs ordered by its physicians? The record shows you have been personally withdrawing small quantities of strophanthin from the pharmacy over the past month. There is no evidence that you were administering the drug to any of your patients at the hospital during that period of time." Carella paused. "We know exactly *how* you did it, Dr. Nelson. Now would you like to tell us *why?*"

Nelson was silent.

"Then perhaps Mrs. Gifford would," Carella said. He walked to the stairwell at the far end of the entry. "Mrs. Gifford," he called, "would you please put on your clothes and come downstairs?"

Elizabeth Rushmore Hospital was on the southern rim of the city, a complex of tall white buildings that faced the River Dix. From the hospital windows, one could watch the river traffic, could see in the distance the smokestacks puffing up black clouds, could follow the spidery strand of the three bridges that connected the island to Sands Spit, Calm's Point, and Majesta.

A cold wind was blowing off the water. He had called the hospital earlier that afternoon and learned that evening visiting hours ended at eight o'clock. It was now seven-forty-five, and he stood on the river's edge with his coat collar raised, and looked up at the lighted hospital windows and once again went over his plan.

He had thought at first that the whole thing was a cheap cop trick. He had listened attentively while Buddy told him about the visit of the blond cop, the same son of a bitch; Buddy said his name was Kling, Detective Bert

Kling. Holding the phone receiver to his ear, he had
listened, and his hand had begun sweating on the black
plastic. But he had told himself all along that it was only a
crumby trick, did they think he was going to fall for such a
cheap stunt?

Still, they had known his name; Kling had asked for
Cookie. How could they have known his name unless
there really *was* a file some place listing guys who were
involved with numbers? And hadn't Kling mentioned something about not being able to locate him at the address they
had for him in the file? If anything sounded legit, that sure
as hell did. He had moved two years ago, so maybe the
file went back before then. And besides, he hadn't been
home for the past few days, so even if the file was a *recent*
one, well then they wouldn't have been able to locate him
at his address because he simply hadn't been there. So
maybe there was some truth in it, who the hell knew?

But a picture? Where would they have gotten a picture
of him? Well, that was maybe possible. If the cops really
did have such a file, then maybe they also had a picture.
He knew goddamn well that they took pictures all the
time, mostly trying to get a line on guys in narcotics, but
maybe they did it for numbers, too. He had seen laundry
trucks or furniture vans parked in the same spot on a street
all day long, and had known—together with everybody
else in the neighborhood—that it was cops taking pictures.
So maybe it was possible they had a picture of him, too.
And maybe that little bitch had really pointed him out,
maybe so, it was a possibility. But it still smelled a little,
there were still too many unanswered questions.

Most of the questions were answered for him when he
read the story in the afternoon paper. He'd almost missed
it because he had started from the back of the paper, where
the racing results were, and then had only turned to the
front afterwards, sort of killing time. The story confirmed
that there *was* a file on numbers racketeers, for one thing,
though he was pretty sure about that even before he'd seen
the paper. It also explained why Fairchild couldn't make
the identification, too. You can't be expected to look at a
picture of somebody when you're laying in the hospital

with a coma. He didn't think he'd hit the bastard that hard, but maybe he didn't know his own strength. Just to check he'd called Buena Vista as soon as he'd read the story and asked how Patrolman Fairchild was doing. They told him he was still in coma and on the critical list, so that part of it was true. And, of course, if those jerks in the office where Cindy worked were too scared to identify the picture, well then Fairchild's condition explained why Cindy was the only person the cops could bank on.

The word "homicide" had scared him. If that son of a bitch *did* die, and if the cops picked him up and Cindy said, yes, that's the man, well, that was it, pal. He thought he'd really made it clear to her, but maybe she was tougher than he thought. For some strange reason, the idea excited him, the idea of her not having been frightened by the beating, of her still having the guts to identify his picture and promise to testify. He could remember being excited when he read the story, and the same excitement overtook him now as he looked up at the hospital windows and went over his plan.

Visiting hours ended at eight o'clock, which meant he had exactly ten minutes to get into the building. He wondered suddenly if they would let him in so close to the deadline, and he immediately began walking toward the front entrance. A wide slanting concrete canopy covered the revolving entrance doors. The hospital was new, an imposing edifice of aluminum and glass and concrete. He pushed through the revolving doors and walked immediately to the desk on the right of the entrance lobby. A woman in white—he supposed she was a nurse—looked up as he approached.

"Miss Cynthia Forrest?" he said.

"Room seven-twenty," the woman said, and immediately looked at her watch. "Visiting hours are over in a few minutes, you know," she said.

"Yes, I know, thanks," he answered, and smiled, and walked swiftly to the elevator bank. There was only one other civilian waiting for an elevator; the rest were all hospital people in white uniforms. He wondered abruptly if there would be a cop on duty outside her door. Well, if there is, he thought, I just call it off, that's all. The elevator doors opened. He stepped in with the other people, pushed the button for the seventh floor, noticed that one of the nurses reached for the same button after he had pushed it, and then withdrew quietly to the rear of the elevator. The doors closed.

"If you ask me," a nurse was saying, "it's psoriasis. Dr. Kirsch said it's blood poisoning, but did you see that man's leg? You can't tell me that's from blood poisoning."

"Well, they're going to test him tomorrow," another nurse said.

"In the meantime, he's got a fever of a hundred and two."

"That's from the swollen leg. The leg's all infected, you know."

"Psoriasis," the first nurse said, "*that's* what it is," and the doors opened. Both nurses stepped out. The doors closed again. The elevator was silent. He looked at his watch. It was five minutes to eight. The elevator stopped again at the fourth floor, and again at the fifth. On the seventh floor, he got off the elevator with the nurse who had earlier reached for the same button. He hesitated in the corridor for a moment. There was a wide-open area directly in front of the elevators. Beyond that was a large room with a bank of windows, the sunroom, he supposed. To the right and left of the elevators were glass doors leading to the patients' rooms beyond. A nurse sat at a desk some three feet before the doors on the left. He walked swiftly to the desk and said, "Which way is seven-twenty?"

The nurse barely looked up. "Straight through," she said. "You've only got a few minutes."

"Yes, I know, thanks," he said, and pushed open the glass door. The room just inside the partition was 700, and the one beyond that was 702, so he assumed 720 was somewhere at the end of the hall. He looked at his watch. It was almost eight o'clock. He hastily scanned the doors in the corridor, walking rapidly, finding the one marked MEN halfway down the hall. Pushing open the door, he walked immediately to one of the stalls, entered it, and locked it behind him.

In less than a minute, he heard a loudspeaker announcing that visiting hours were now over. He smiled, lowered the toilet seat, sat, lighted a cigarette, and began his long wait.

He did not come out of the men's room until midnight. By that time, he had listened to a variety of patients and doctors as they discussed an endless variety of ills and ailments, both subjectively and objectively. He listened to each of them quietly and with some amusement because they helped to pass the time. He had reasoned that he could not make his move until the hospital turned out the lights in all the rooms. He didn't know what time taps was in this crumby place, but he supposed it would be around ten or ten-thirty. He had decided to wait until midnight, just to be sure. He figured that all of the visiting doctors would be gone by that time, and so he knew he had to be careful when he came out into the corridor. He didn't want anyone to stop him or even to see him on the way to Cindy's room.

It was a shame he would have to kill the little bitch.

She could have really been something.

There was a guy who came back to pee a total of seventeen times between eight o'clock and midnight. He knew because the guy was evidently having some kind of kidney trouble, and every time he came into the john he would walk over to the urinals—the sound of his shuffling slippers carrying into the locked stall—and then he would begin cursing out loud while he peed, "Oh, you son of a bitch! Oh, what did I do to deserve such pain and misery?" and like that. One time, while he was peeing, some other guy yelled out from the stall alongside, "For God's sake, Mandel, keep your sickness to yourself."

And then the guy standing at the urinals had yelled back, "It should happen to *you*, Liebowitz! It should *rot*, and fall off of you, and be washed down the drain into the river, may God hear my plea!"

He had almost burst out laughing, but instead he lighted another cigarette and looked at his watch again, and wondered what time they'd be putting all these sick jerks to bed, and wondered what Cindy would be wearing. He could still remember her undressing that night he'd beat her up, the quick flash of her nudity—he stopped his thoughts. He could not think that way. He had to kill her tonight, there was no sense thinking about—and yet maybe *while* he was doing it, maybe it would be like last time, maybe with her belly smooth and hard beneath him, maybe like last time maybe he could.

The men's room was silent at midnight.

He unlocked the stall and came out into the room and then walked past the sinks to the door and opened it just a bit and looked out into the corridor. The floors were some kind of hard polished asphalt tile, and you could hear the clicking of high heels on it for a mile, which was good. He listened as a nurse went swiftly down the corridor, her heels clicking away, and then he listened until everything was quiet again. Quickly, he stepped out into the hall. He began walking toward the end of the corridor, the steadily mounting door numbers flashing by on left and right, 709, 710, 711 . . . 714, 715, 716 . . .

He was passing the door to room 717 on his left, when it opened and a nurse stepped into the corridor. He was too startled to speak at first. He stopped dead, breathless, debating whether he should hit her. And then, from somewhere, he heard a voice saying, "Good evening, nurse," and he hardly recognized the voice as his own because it sounded so cultured and pleasant and matter-of-fact. The nurse looked at him for just a moment longer, and then smiled and said, "Good evening, doctor," and continued walking down the corridor. He did not turn to look back at her. He continued walking until he came to room 720. Hoping it was a private room, he opened the door, stepped inside quickly, closed the door immediately, and leaned against it, listening. He could hear nothing in the corridor outside. Satisfied, he turned into the room.

The only light in the room came from the windows at the far end, just beyond the bed. He could see the silhouette of her body beneath the blankets, the curved hip limned by the dim light coming from the window. The blanket was pulled high over her shoulders and the back of her neck, but he could see the short blond hair illuminated by the dim glow of moonlight from the windows. He was getting excited again, the way he had that night he beat her up. He reminded himself why he was here—this girl could send him to the electric chair. If Fairchild died, the girl was all they needed to convict him. He took a deep breath and moved toward the bed.

In the near-darkness, he reached for her throat, seized it between his huge hands and then whispered, "Cindy," because he wanted her to be awake and looking straight up into his face when he crushed the life out of her. His hands tightened.

She sat erect suddenly. Two fists flew up between his own hands, up and outward, breaking the grip. His eyes opened wide.

"Surprise!" Bert Kling said, and punched him in the mouth.

11

Detectives are not poets; there is no iambic pentameter in a broken head.

If Meyer were William Shakespeare, he might have indeed believed that "Love is a smoke raised with the fume of sighs," but he wasn't William Shakespeare. If Steve Carella were Henry Wadsworth Longfellow, he would have known that "Love is ever busy with his shuttle," but alas, you know, he wasn't Henry Wadsworth Longfellow—though he did have an Uncle Henry who lived in Red Bank, New Jersey. As a matter of fact, if either of the two men were Buckingham or Ovid or Byron, they might have respectively realized that "love is the salt of life," and "the perpetual source of fears and anxieties," and "a capricious power"—but they weren't poets, they were only working cops.

Even as working cops, they might have appreciated Homer's comment (from the motion picture of the same name) which, translated into English subtitles by Nikos Konstantin, went something like this: *"Who love too much, hate in the like extreme."*

But they had neither seen the picture nor read the book, what the hell can you expect from flatfoots?

Oh, they could tell you tales of love, all right. Boy, the tales of love they could tell. They had heard tales of love from a hundred and one people, or maybe even more. And don't think they didn't know what love was all about, oh, they knew what it was all about, all right. Love was sweet and pure and marvelous, love was magnificent. Hadn't they loved their mothers and their fathers and their aunts and uncles and such? Hadn't they kissed a girl for the first time when they were thirteen or fourteen or something, wasn't that love? Oh boy, it sure was. And weren't they both happily married men who loved their wives and their children? Listen, it wouldn't pay to tell them about love because they knew all about it, yes, sir.

"We love each other," Nelson said.

"We love each other," Melanie said.

The pair sat in the 2:00 A.M. silence of the squadroom and dictated their confessions to police stenographers, sitting at separate desks, their hands still stained with the ink that had been used to fingerprint them. Meyer and Carella listened unemotionally, silently, patiently—they had heard it all before. Neither Nelson nor Melanie seemed to realize that they would be taken from the precinct by police van at 9:00 A.M, brought downtown for arraignment, and then put into separate cells. They had been seeing each other secretly for more than a year, they said, but they did not yet seem to realize they would not see each other again until they were brought to trial—and then perhaps never after.

Carella and Meyer listened silently as their tale of love unfolded.

"You can't legislate against love," Nelson said, transforming another man's comment, but making his meaning clear enough. "This thing between Melanie and me just happened. Neither of us wanted it, and neither of us asked for it. It just happened."

"It just happened," Melanie said at the desk nearby. "I remember exactly when. We were sitting outside the studio in Carl's car one night, waiting for Stan to take off his makeup so the three of us could go to dinner together. Carl's hand touched mine, and the next thing we knew we were kissing. We fell in love shortly afterwards. I guess we fell in love."

"We fell in love," Nelson said. "We tried to stop ourselves. We knew it wasn't right. But when we saw we couldn't stop, we went to Stan and told him about it, and asked him for a divorce. This was immediately after the incident at his party, when he tried to hit me. Last month, September. We told him we were in love and that Melanie wanted a divorce. He flatly refused.''

"I think he'd known about us all along," Melanie said. "If you say he revised his will, then that's why he must have done it. He must have known that Carl and I were having an affair. He was a very sensitive man, my husband. He must have known that something was wrong long before we told him about it.''

"The idea to kill him was mine," Nelson said.

"I agreed to it readily," Melanie said.

"I began drawing strophanthin from the hospital pharmacy last month. I know the pharmacist there, I often stop in when I'm short of something or other, something I need in my bag or at my office. I'll stop in and say, 'Hi, Charlie, I need some penicillin,' and of course he'll give it to me because he knows me. I did the same thing with the strophanthin. I never discussed why I needed it. I assumed he thought it was for my private practice, outside the hospital. At any rate, he never questioned me about it, why should he?''

"Carl prepared the capsule," Melanie said. "At the breakfast table that Wednesday, after Stan had taken his morning vitamins, I switched the remaining capsule for the one containing the poison. At lunch, I watched while he washed it down with water. We knew it would take somewhere between three and eight hours for the capsule to dissolve, but we didn't know exactly how long. We didn't necessarily expect him to die on camera, but it didn't matter, you see. We'd be nowhere near when it happened, and that was all that mattered. We'd be completely out of it.''

"And yet," Nelson said, "we realized that I would be a prime suspect. After all, I am a physician, and I do have access to drugs. We planned for this possibility by making certain that *I* was the one who suggested foul play, *I* was the one who demanded an autopsy.''

"We also figured," Melanie said, "that it would be a good idea if I said I suspected Carl. Then, once you found

out what kind of poison had been used—how fast it worked,
I mean—and once you knew Carl had been home all
during the show, well then you'd automatically drop him
as a suspect. That was what we figured."

"We love each other," Nelson said.

"We love each other," Melanie said.

They sat still and silent after they had finished talking.
The police stenographers showed them transcripts of what
they had separately said, and they signed multiple copies,
and then Alf Miscolo came out of the Clerical Office,
handcuffed the pair, and led them downstairs to the deten-
tion cells.

"One for us, one for the lieutenant, and one for Homicide," Carella told his stenographer. The stenographer
merely nodded. He, too, had heard it all already. There
was nothing you could tell him about love or homicide. He
put on his hat, dropped the requested number of signed
confessions on the desk nearest the railing, and went out
of the squadroom. As he walked down the corridor, he could
hear muted voices behind the closed door of the Interrogation Room.

"Why'd you beat her up?" Kling asked.

"I didn't beat up nobody," Cookie said. "I love that
girl."

"You *what?*"

"I love her, you deaf? I loved her from the first minute
I ever seen her."

"When was that?"

"The end of the summer. August. It was on the Stem. I
just made a collection in a candy store on the corner there,
and I was passing this Pokerino place in the middle of the
block, and I thought maybe I'd stop in, kill some time,
you know? The guy outside was giving his spiel, and I was
standing there listening to him, so many games for a
quarter, or whatever the hell it was. I looked in and there
was this girl in a dark-green dress, leaning over one of the
tables and rolling the balls, I think she had something like
three queens, I'm not sure."

"All right, what happened then?"

"I went in."

"Go ahead."

"What do you want from me?"

"I want to know why you beat her up."

"I didn't beat her up, I told you that!"

"Who'd you think was in that bed tonight, you son of a bitch?"

"I didn't *know* who was in it. Leave me alone. You got nothing on me, you think I'm some snot-nosed kid?"

"Yeah, I think you're some snot-nosed kid," Kling said. "What happened that first night you saw her?"

"Nothing. There was a guy with her, a young guy, one of these advertising types. I kept watching her, that's all. She didn't know I was watching her, she didn't even know I existed. Then I followed them when they left, and found out where she lived, and after that I kept following her wherever she went. That's all."

"That's *not* all."

"I'm telling you that's all."

"Okay, play it your way," Kling said. "Be a wise guy. We'll throw everything but the goddamn kitchen sink at you."

"I'm telling you I never laid a finger on her. I went up to her office to let her know, that's all."

"Let her know what?"

"That she was my girl. That, you know, she wasn't supposed to go out with nobody else or see nobody, that she was *mine*, you dig? That's the only reason I went up there, to let her know. I didn't expect all that kind of goddamn trouble. All I wanted to do was tell her what I expected from her, that's all."

John "Cookie" Cacciatore lowered his head. The brim of the hat hid his eyes from Kling's gaze.

"If you'd all have minded your own business, everything would have been all right."

The squadroom was silent.

"I love that girl," he said.

And then, in a mumble, "You lousy bastard, you almost killed me tonight."

Morning always comes.

In the morning, Detective Bert Kling went to Elizabeth

Rushmore Hospital and asked to see Cynthia Forrest. He knew this was not the normal visiting time, but he explained that he was a working detective, and asked that an allowance be made. Since everyone in the hospital knew that he was the cop who'd captured a hoodlum on the seventh floor the night before, there was really no need to explain. Permission was granted at once.

Cindy was sitting up in bed.

She turned her head toward the door as Kling came in, and then her hand went unconsciously to her short blond hair, fluffing it.

"Hi," he said.

"Hello."

"How do you feel?"

"All right." She touched her eyes gingerly. "Has the swelling gone down?"

"Yes."

"But they're still discolored, aren't they?"

"Yes, they are. You look all right, though."

"Thank you." Cindy paused. "Did . . . did he hurt you last night?"

"No."

"You're sure."

"Yes, I'm sure."

"He's a vicious person."

"I know he is."

"Will he go to jail?"

"To prison, yes. Even without your testimony. He assaulted a police officer." Kling smiled. "Tried to strangle me, in fact. That's attempted murder."

"I'm . . . I'm very frightened of that man," Cindy said.

"Yes, I can imagine."

"But . . ." She swallowed. "But if it'll help the case, I'll . . . I'd be willing to testify. If it'll help, I mean."

"I don't know," Kling said. "The d.a.'s office'll have to let us know about that."

"All right," Cindy said, and was silent. Sunlight streamed through the windows, catching her blond hair. She lowered her eyes. Her hand picked nervously at the blanket.

"The only thing I'm afraid of is . . . is when he gets out. Eventually, I mean. When he gets out."

"Well, we'll see that you have police protection," Kling said.

"Mmm," Cindy said. She did not seem convinced.

"I mean . . . I'll *personally* volunteer for the job," Kling said, and hesitated.

Cindy raised her eyes to meet his. "That's . . . very kind of you," she said slowly.

"Well . . ." he answered, and shrugged.

The room was silent.

"You could have got hurt last night," Cindy said.

"No. No, there wasn't a chance."

"You could have," she insisted.

"No, really."

"Yes," she said.

"We're not going to start arguing again, are we?"

"No," she said, and laughed, and then winced and touched her face. "Oh, God," she said, "it still hurts."

"But only when you laugh, right?"

"Yes," she said, and laughed again.

"When do you think you'll be out of here?" Kling asked.

"I don't know. Tomorrow, I suppose. Or the day after."

"Because I thought . . ."

"Yes?"

"Well . . ."

"What is it, Detective Kling?"

"I know you're a working girl . . ."

"Yes?"

"And that you don't normally eat out."

"That's right, I don't," Cindy said.

"Unless you're escorted."

Cindy waited.

"I thought . . ."

She waited.

"I thought you'd like to have dinner with me sometime. When you're out of the hospital, I mean." He shrugged.

"I mean, *I'd* pay for it," Kling said, and lapsed into silence.

Cindy did not answer for several moments. Then she smiled and said simply, "I'd love to," and paused, and immediately said, "When?"

SENSATIONAL
87TH PRECINCT NOVELS
FROM THE GRAND MASTER
ED MCBAIN

LULLABY   70384-X/$4.95 US/$5.95 Can
A wealthy young couple has returned home from a New Year's
Eve party to discover their babysitter and her infant charge
savagely murdered.

TRICKS   70383-1/$3.95 US/$4.95 Can
It's Halloween night and hell has opened its gates on the 87th
Precinct. It's all tricks and no treats, including surprise
packages from a killer who specializes in body parts.

POISON   70030-1/$3.95 US/$4.95 Can
"Sums up the hot-wire style that has kept McBain ahead of the
competition for three decades."   *Philadelphia Inquirer*

EIGHT BLACK HORSES   70029-8/$3.95 US/$4.95 Can
A series of bizarre clues signals the return of the Deaf Man—
who this time intends to exact his full measure of revenge.

LIGHTNING   69974-5/$4.50 US/$5.50 Can
The compelling new novel in the 87th Precinct series, where
the dedicated men and women who wear the gold badge push
themselves to the limit of danger.

ICE   67108-5$4.50 US/$5.50 Can
"In the rough and raunchy world of the 87th Precinct...a half-
dozen murders—including a magnificent piece of street
justice—keep nerves jangling."   *Philadelphia Inquirer*

POLICE THRILLERS by
"THE ACKNOWLEDGED MASTER"
Newsweek

ED McBAIN

CALYPSO	70591-5/$3.50 US/$4.50 Can
DOLL	70082-4/$4.50 US/$5.50 Can
THE MUGGER	70081-6/$3.50 US/$4.50 Can
HE WHO HESITATES	70084-0/$3.50 US/$4.50 Can
KILLER'S CHOICE	70083-2/$3.50 US/$4.50 Can
BREAD	70368-8/$4.50 US/$5.50 Can
80 MILLION EYES	70367-X/$4.50 US/$5.50 Can
HAIL TO THE CHIEF	70370-X/$4.50 US/$5.50 Can
LONG TIME NO SEE	70369-6/$3.50 US/$4.50 Can

Don't Miss These Other
Exciting Novels

DOORS	70371-8/$3.50 US/$4.50 Can
WHERE THERE'S SMOKE	70372-6/$3.50 US/$4.50 Can
GUNS	70373-4/$3.50 US/$4.50 Can
GANGS!	70757-8/$3.50 US/$4.25 Can
THE SENTRIES	70489-7/$3.50 US/$4.50 Can